Merrow

Other  titles

Louise Cooper
Merrow

Hodder
Children's
Books

A division of Hodder Headline Limited

This is for Robyn Holroyd, with grateful thanks
for (1) lending me her name and
(2) expertly checking my street cred!

'Thanks to that wonderful device called
Author's Licence, this story is set in a version
of St. Ives that is partly real and partly
pure imagination. I leave it to you to
decide which is which.'

Louise Cooper, 2005

One

Robyn's probably managed to find the only windproof spot on the entire beach. I can see her over there, near the furthest cliff spur; that turquoise towel of hers is pretty unmistakable. Looks as if she's sunbathing, but every now and then she lifts her head and glances at the sea. I'd take any bet that there's a pencil in her hand and she's sketching something. Or someone. No prizes for guessing who.

The lifeguards are packing up. They've taken down the flags and are hauling the rescue boards back towards the surf clubhouse. Must be gone six, then. Feels earlier; I haven't got used to the fact that it's nearly midsummer and the days are so much longer. All the visitors have gone, too. There were quite a few visitors around today – it's getting to the time of year when they start to outnumber the locals. I saw a couple of amazing-looking girls earlier. One of them smiled at me; it was a come-on, no doubt of it. Yeah, well. More fool me for not taking her up on the offer . . .

I suppose I could go in again; but I can't really be bothered. All the hassle of getting my wetsuit back on, and anyway, the surf's getting messy now, with that crosswind. Maybe I'll walk over and see what Robyn's doing. Just curiosity; that's all . . .

Robyn had felt pleasantly hot in her cranny among the rocks, but in the past half-hour the wind had freshened, and now when it gusted it caused a sharp chill along the length of her spine which was starting to get annoying. The sheet of paper in front of her kept lifting and flapping; she had anchored it with one elbow, but that made her drawing angle awkward and her wrist was starting to ache as a result. So she gave up, putting the pencil down and resting her chin on folded arms as she stared through damp, red-gold strands of hair along the quarter-mile length of the beach. Three people were still surfing at this end, but they were the last, the die-hards; the sea was pretty rough now and waves were breaking every which way and piling one on top of another, making it nearly impossible to get a good run. Robyn's own longboard lay beside her, upside down with its keel standing proud like a bright-yellow shark's fin and her wetsuit draped over it. The tide was coming in fast; have to move soon, or one of those sudden surges could catch her out . . .

She felt the change of temperature as a shadow fell across her, and turned her head, squinting against the bright sky.

'Oh, hi, Jay. You OK?'

'Yeah, good.' Jay Trehane (he did not like his full name of Jeremy, and didn't use it unless forced to) smiled at her through his salty and wind-ruffled fringe. Robyn smiled back, then nodded at the pile of her belongings on the far side of the surfboard.

'Pass my fleece over, would you? I'm getting cold.'

He passed it; she moved over on the towel to allow him to sit down beside her, and he peered at the unfinished sketch, partly obscured now by her arms. It showed a single figure on a longboard, half-crouched, dark hair flying, as a dramatically large wave curled and broke around him. 'That's good,' Jay said.

'Not really. The head's out of proportion, and no one ever stands on a board exactly like that.'

'Not even Kiran?'

She laughed. 'Well, maybe. But I'm not going to show him this. He'd laugh.' She shoved the sketch under a corner of the towel and turned her attention to the sea again. Then, abruptly alert, she sat up. 'Hey, look – there's a good wave rising; see it, further out? Kiran's there; he should catch it!'

One of the three surfers had given up and was wading out, but the other two had turned their boards and were paddling towards the slowly rising wave.

'Yeah!' Robyn was half on her feet, eyes fixed on the taller of the two surfers. 'Come on, Kiran, go for it!'

Both surfers were in time to turn and catch the wave as it towered to a peak and began to curl over. White foam crashed and boiled, the wind flinging a crest of spray up and out like a horse's flying mane.

'Oh, wow, look at *that*!' Robyn's voice rose delightedly as the pair emerged from the maelstrom, riding shorewards at breathtaking speed. Then she shrieked with laughter as one board swerved and flipped and its rider, arms and legs windmilling, took an inglorious header into the sea.

'*Cool!* I wish I had a camera – I could blackmail him for years with a shot of that!' Sobering, she grinned at Jay. 'Got to admit he's good, though.'

Jay nodded. Kiran had surfaced, shaking his head, and as the wave petered out in the shallows he waded after it, towing his board behind him and emerging from the water. Robyn waved, and he veered towards them.

'Nice one!' she said drolly, as he reached them.

'Thanks a bunch!' Kiran flopped down on the towel, dripping all over the other two. He was taller than Jay, more muscular, his dark hair longer; and even this early in the summer his skin was enviably brown. 'It's getting pretty lousy out there, now,' he added by way of explanation.

'Don't make excuses,' said Robyn. She looped an arm around his neck and kissed him. Kiran didn't respond to the kiss, but glanced at Jay and raised his eyebrows expressively. Then he asked, 'Either of you got anything to eat?'

Jay said no, and Robyn said, 'You're a pig, you'll get fat. And move over; you're soaking everything.' She was ebullient, excited, the way she always was with him, and Jay looked away, feeling uncomfortable. In the three months since Kiran and Robyn had become an 'item', of sorts, being around them was increasingly difficult. It wasn't that they excluded him – at least, Kiran didn't – but the easy balance of their old three-cornered friendship had changed, and Jay felt more and more like an unwanted hanger-on. It wasn't that he had no other friends. He had grown up here, was part of the surf scene: in a place like this no one went short of friends. But the fact that it was Kiran and Robyn . . .

She's not his type, not long-term. She's creative, artistic, a dreamer like me. Kiran might have a great brain, but he's about as sensitive as a torpedo. He's too brash for her. But she's crazy about him, and she's trying to be like him, trying to turn herself into what she thinks he wants. It can't work. Sooner or later, she's going to get hurt. And I don't want that . . .

'Look, I think I'll head home.' Without consciously realizing it, Jay had got to his feet. He felt restless and potentially miserable, and he didn't want either of them to know it. He looked seawards, blinking against the sun. 'I've got a few things to do, so . . .'

The sentence tailed off and he stood very still, staring.

Kiran was rubbing sand off his longboard and did not notice Jay's sudden tension. Robyn, though, was more observant.

'What's up?' she said, sharply. 'What are you looking at?'

Jay didn't answer but moved out of the lee of the rocks and a few paces along the sand. 'Oh-oh . . .' he said.

'*What*, for crying out loud?' Curiosity, impatience, and now a hint of concern were mixed in Robyn's tone, and she too stood up. Her eyes followed the direction of his stare. 'Oh, I don't believe it! Who *is* that idiot?' Jumping on the spot, she waved her arms and shouted, 'Hey! Hey, you! Don't you know the tide's coming in? *Get back!*'

She started to run towards the sea's edge. From the towel, Kiran called out, 'What's going on?'

Jay's head flicked round. 'There's some cretinous tourist climbing around on the Finger!' He started after Robyn, who was knee-deep in the water now, still shouting and waving.

'Bloody hell!' Kiran caught him up and they joined Robyn. 'Is she blind, or just stupid?'

At the end of the beach, about thirty metres from where they stood, the long outcrop of rocks known locally as the Finger jutted into the sea. The rocks were encrusted with mussels and barnacles, and slippery clumps of wrack grew from crevices and made the surface treacherous. A dark-haired girl was on the outcrop, moving unsteadily towards the seaward end. Both her arms were spread wide in an effort to balance, but her movements were hampered by a long coat that flapped around her as her feet slipped and scrambled. The Finger was already half-submerged as the tide came in; waves slapped powerfully less than a metre below the girl, and surf was breaking over the rocks just a short way ahead of her.

'*Hey!*' Kiran joined his voice to Robyn's in a bellow. '*Get off there! Come back!*'

Robyn said, 'She can't hear us!'

'I think she can.' Jay's heartbeat had gone up a good few notches and he had a sudden, ugly sense of premonition. He looked quickly over his shoulder. The beach was deserted, the lifeguard post closed up. One vehicle in the car park, but that probably belonged to the family party with two dogs who were walking up the further cliff path. Beach shop shut, no one visible around the clifftop chalets or at the big Edwardian hotel on the headland. No one to call on, no one else to help.

Kiran said sharply, 'I'm going after her.' He started to run towards the rocks, and for an instant Jay had an urge to go with him. But common sense intervened and instead he swung round and sprinted up the beach towards the surf club. Robyn dithered, torn between the need to help and a surge of fear for Kiran's safety. But Kiran was already clambering up to the spine of the rocks; and the girl had reached the end of the promontory.

Robyn made a decision, and ran after Jay.

She was halfway to the clubhouse when she heard a yell from behind her. Terrified of what she might see, she slid to a halt and swung round.

Kiran was nearly halfway along the Finger, but he had stopped moving and was crouching motionless on the rock. The girl had reached the very end of the outcrop, and had turned to face him. She, too, was motionless, and there was something challenging in the way she stood, feet braced, body tense, the loose coat flapping now like tattered wings, and her face a pale blur under wind-whipped hair. Kiran was shaking his head desperately; he raised one arm, beckoning, almost pleading.

The girl stared at him a moment longer. Then in one fluid movement she turned and jumped from the rock into the sea.

'*NO!*' Kiran's horrified shout rose above the noise of the surf, and Robyn's own scream reverberated in her ears. Kiran was scrabbling back over the rocks; seeing her, he gestured frantically towards the clubhouse, and Robyn raced blindly towards it. Jay had already reached it; it was locked, but they all knew how to trick the lock, and when Robyn arrived he was dragging out one of the big rescue boards. She grabbed one end and between them they manhandled the board at a staggering run back to the sea.

Kiran had retrieved his own longboard and was powering through the surf on it, lying flat and paddling with all his strength. Jay and Robyn plunged after him; a breaker hit the rescue board broadside and almost tore it out of their grasp, but they managed to right it and heaved themselves on. Without wetsuits the sea felt shockingly cold; Jay, in front, was half-blinded by spray, and every wave that broke over the board's prow gave him a gagging, stinging mouthful of water. Kiran was shouting something, but they could not hear him. All they could do was follow where he led, towards the spot where the girl had jumped. They all knew that the chances of even glimpsing her were virtually nil; a big current was running and would sweep her away fast. But Kiran, heading for the rocks, suddenly raised one arm in a wild signal – and an instant later, a shriek from Robyn dinned in Jay's ear.

'There she is!'

A dark thing in the water, shapeless, tossing; it could as easily have been a clump of seaweed torn loose from its mooring and carried in on the tide. But Jay saw the dark thing twist suddenly – and for one shocking moment a human face showed between the rocks and the surging tide.

Kiran had almost reached the girl. Clinging to his board with one hand, he stretched out the other in a desperate effort to get hold of her. He missed;

a wave broke, churning, turned the board at a dizzying angle and lifted it away from the rocks as if it were a matchstick. The dark shape rose, too; Kiran had no chance to plan any move, but his hand clawed out again, instinctively, and Robyn shrieked a second time as she saw his fingers lock on to the collar of the girl's coat.

For one moment Jay really believed that Kiran would do it. He was pulling the girl up against the drag of the tide and her clothing, arm muscles standing out with the strain of hauling. Then, with the rescue board only a metre away and Robyn already reaching to help, the girl gave another twist. Her arms flailed high out of the water; one hand, splay-fingered, clawed savagely at Kiran's eyes, and the other clamped on his ankle and pulled. Taken completely by surprise, Kiran was jerked off-balance; the board rose again on the swell, carrying him and the girl with it – then Kiran lost his grip and, flailing, pitched headlong into the sea.

Jay lurched sideways as a crosscurrent buffeted the rescue board and swung it round. As he tried to get it under control Robyn sprang to a crouch, then the board bucked violently as she dived from it and struck out strongly towards the two figures in the water. The girl's arms were clamped round Kiran's neck and she was dragging him under with her. Robyn reached them; her clasped hands thrust between the girl's arms, then snapped up and out, breaking the stranglehold. Kiran came up with a bubbling inrush of breath, but the girl was fighting like a rabid animal, and even between them they couldn't hold her. Jay could do nothing to help them; all his energy was concentrated on the struggle to control the board as the tide threatened to smash it, and him, on to the rocks. Then he heard a sound that curdled his stomach – a cry from Kiran, horrified, despairing, as another wave broke against the Finger and the backwash snatched the girl out of his grasp. Within a second she was three metres away; two seconds more and her shape slid beneath the water's surface and vanished.

'No!' Robyn screamed. 'No, *no!*'

'Robyn!' Jay fought to guide the rescue board to where she bobbed like a cork, but Kiran reached her first. Towing her with him, he gripped one of the board's grab-handles and heaved her up, then kicked powerfully and scrambled aboard behind Jay. Robyn doubled over, coughing water, and Jay and Kiran turned the board towards the shore. Kiran's longboard had vanished but no one gave it a thought. All that mattered was to get back to the beach and raise the alarm.

The sun vanished behind a cloud as they surfed in, and a wing of shadow swept the length of the beach like an omen, dulling the light to chill grey. Kiran jumped off the board and ran to where Robyn had left her things; as Jay helped Robyn to her feet and followed, Kiran had already found her mobile and was calling the emergency services.

'Coastguard!' Kiran's breath was rasping in his throat and his chest heaved. Seconds passed like hours as he was put through. 'Yeah, Coastguard? A woman's been washed off a rock at Craster Beach – we tried to get to her, but she was swept away . . . Outcrop called the Finger, eastern end of the beach . . . About five minutes ago . . . What? Oh – Mason; Kiran Mason . . . No, I'm not; they'd packed up and gone before it happened . . . Yeah, we'll be here . . . Right. Thanks.'

He cut the connection, then squatted on the sand, folding his arms on his knees and pressing his forehead against them.

'You all right?' Jay asked.

Kiran nodded without looking up. 'They're calling out the inshore lifeboat. Not much point though, is there?' His voice was muffled and his tone flat with shock.

Jay felt unreal; he turned to look for Robyn and saw her standing at the sea's edge, staring down at the wavelets that petered out around her feet. Then beyond the far headland an orange trail snaked skywards and flared dazzlingly. A second followed on its heels, and the double *bang* of the lifeboat maroons echoed across the beach. Gulls answered raucously, and somewhere in the far distance a dog started barking.

As the echoes faded and the gulls settled, Jay stared at the maroons' smoke trails dissipating above the hotel. Everything looked so *normal*, as if no disaster had happened, or ever could, in such a peaceful setting. He felt helpless, confused, bereft. Then Robyn's head came up, and the look in her eyes brought him back to earth. She stared at him as if she couldn't quite remember who he was. She was shivering and, thankful for any small thing to do, Jay picked up her towel and took it to her, wrapping it round her shoulders.

'Lifeboat's on its way,' he said, indistinctly.

'Yeah.' She nodded. 'God, Jay, we so *nearly* got her . . .'

'I know.'

'Is Kiran all right?'

Jay looked. Kiran was sitting down now, head still between his knees, and the sand damp around him.

'He'll be OK,' Jay said. 'Just shocked, I think.'

Another nod, but she said nothing else, and Jay couldn't think of any words that wouldn't sound crass. The cloud had passed and the deserted beach was bright with sunlight once more. It all seemed very incongruous. Jay's mind kept pulling him back, trying to conjure images of the girl in the water. He pushed the mental pictures away, repelled by them and aware, too, that he was starting to feel extremely sick. *Lifeboat should arrive soon. Coastguards, too; probably be a toss-up which lot gets here first. Should we call anyone else? Robyn's brother Greg is a lifeguard. Probably get him on his mobile. Or maybe Mum and Dad. Why do I suddenly want to talk to someone?*

The sound of vehicle engines brought Jay back to earth, and when he looked up he saw a four-wheel drive in the dark-blue coastguard livery crossing the car park and bumping down the slope to the sand. An ambulance was parking up behind it; then the four-wheel drive's passenger door opened and a uniformed figure got out and peered across the beach, shading his eyes. Jay raised an arm and the oastguard strode towards him, covering the ground fast.

They knew most of the coastguards, but this face was unfamiliar; possibly, Jay thought, he was new to the area. 'Kiran Mason?' the man asked.

'That's Kiran.' Jay pointed. 'He made the call. But we were all here.'

'We tried,' said Robyn in a small voice. 'We did. We honestly *did*.'

'I know, love, I know.' The coastguard was middle-aged and wind-tanned, with a calm voice and faded-blue eyes which he now fixed on Jay. 'The missing woman – the caller said she was carried up coast?'

'Yes.' Jay's voice caught and he cleared his throat. 'We saw her on the rocks, over there; we went in after her, but—'

'All right; we don't need all the details now; you can tell us when you feel better.' The faded eyes narrowed. 'You're surfers? Local?'

'Yes.'

'So you know the tides and currents?'

Jay nodded, hoping to God that the churning in his stomach was just a passing thing and he wouldn't throw up. 'There's not much chance of finding her,' he heard himself saying. 'I mean, it's spring tides. And it all happened so *fast* . . .'

'Yes, I understand. And I don't doubt you did what you could.' Over Robyn's slumped shoulders the coastguard spotted something; Jay looked too and saw the local Atlantic-class inshore lifeboat curving in fast from the open sea, with its wake churning white and vivid behind it. Abruptly he felt that everything inside him was crumpling and collapsing, as if something had gathered all his organs in an unpleasant grip and squeezed them.

''Scuse me . . .' he said indistinctly. 'I think I'm going to chuck . . .'

He managed to get behind a rock before the mixture of food and seawater came up, which salved at least a little of his dignity. When he returned, Robyn and the coastguard had walked across to where Kiran sat, and Kiran was looking up at them with hollow, empty eyes. Robyn crouched and put an arm round him, pressing her cheek against his shoulder. The coastguard was talking; Jay wasn't close enough to catch what he said, but he heard Kiran's reply.

But he doesn't sound like Kiran. He sounds like someone else, a stranger, someone I don't know.

Kiran said, 'I saw her face. Before I lost her – she looked straight into my eyes.' He sucked in breath, coughed, shuddered. His eyes had lost their focus and Jay had the disconcerting feeling that he was seeing something none of the rest of them could share.

Kiran said again: 'I saw her *face*.'

Two

I kind of wish I hadn't come tonight. Kind of . . . though in another way it was probably the only sane thing to do. Scenario: Greg and Jodie's flat (that's Robyn's brother Greg; Jodie's his girlfriend). It was Jodie's idea to hold a party to celebrate the end of everyone's exams. She's at uni, and a lot of the people here are older than me; her and Greg's friends. But Jodie's cool; she widened the whole thing to include the rest of us who are still at school or sixth-form college. Like she said, exams are exams whether they're GCSEs or degree finals; we're all in the same boat and we all need to chill. So here we are. Thanks, guys. Really appreciate it.

But it's only been two weeks since the thing happened that we don't talk about and try not to think about. And it's crazily hot tonight, and I'm sitting on the floor under the open window, and somehow the whole atmosphere isn't quite right. The music's too quiet. No one's dancing. No one's doing anything, really.

Robyn and Kiran aren't speaking to each other. Correction: what I should have said is, Kiran isn't speaking to Robyn. She's tried, God knows she's tried, to the point where just about everyone's noticed that she's making a total idiot of herself. But he doesn't respond. And he's getting royally pissed; not drinking beer like the rest of us, but something a lot stronger. Trouble is, no one can do the friendship thing and quietly warn him that he's overdoing it. At the best of times that's not something Kiran tolerates, from anyone, and when he gets like this . . . well, let's just say he's bigger than me, and fitter, and faster, and I'm not about to take the risk. Not even for Robyn's sake.

Jay stared over his drawn-up knees at the party scene, slowly twisting an untouched can of Red Stripe between his palms. He didn't like lager much, but someone had pressed it into his hand and as yet he hadn't found a convenient surface to leave it on – barring the floor, where it would only get knocked over. Outside he could hear the sea in the distance, sounding louder than usual because of the stillness. There wasn't even a breeze tonight. It was rare for the Cornish coast to feel oppressive, but that was the only word he could think of that fitted. Oppressive, and vaguely ominous, as though the world was waiting for something unpleasant to happen. *Probably be the grandfather of all thunderstorms before long,* he told himself, trying to rationalize. But truthfully he knew it wasn't just that. Something else was the trouble. Something that was bugging him and refused to go away.

He looked covertly around for Robyn, and saw her standing in the kitchen doorway, holding the jamb and swinging herself aimlessly from side to side. She was smiling, but the smile didn't fool Jay. It was a mask, a pretence that she was enjoying herself. Her gaze strayed time and again to Kiran, who was kneeling on the floor, going through a pile of CDs and throwing them aside one after another. Everything about Kiran radiated tight, barely-controlled anger. Someone, passing, said something to him but he ignored them, just as he was ignoring Robyn.

Robyn gave up. Jay watched her disappear into the kitchen, counted half a minute so that his motive would be less obvious, and followed.

The kitchen was a mess of plastic glasses, empty bottles and cans, pizza crusts and French bread and cheese crumbs. A couple were doing something intimate against the door of the fridge-freezer, someone else was asleep on a chair, head lolling back and mouth open, and a small, dark-haired girl whom Jay didn't know was making a half-hearted effort to put some of the rubbish in a bin-bag. Robyn was at the sink. She had her back to Jay and he knew that she was trying to pretend she wasn't crying. He went up to her.

'Robyn . . . you OK?'

Stupid question. She turned quickly, defensively. Her make-up had run, and dark smudges round her eyes made her look like a panda.

'Yeah,' she said. 'Hay fever.'

Sure, it is. Jay screwed up his courage and decided to jump in feet first. 'What's the matter with Kiran?'

In the living room the music had stopped and, though it had not been loud, the sudden silence was noticeable. Robyn looked away and shrugged. 'How should I know? He isn't talking to me.'

'Is it the same thing again?'

Another shrug. 'Probably.'

He let out a sharp, angry breath. 'It's a lousy excuse to behave that like to you! You went through it as well; Kiran seems to forget that when it suits him.'

Robyn was saved from replying by a deafening blast of heavy metal from the hi-fi. Voices went up in protest: 'Kiran!' 'Shit, man, turn it down!' 'Turn it *off*!'

The noise stopped as abruptly as it had started, then Kiran could be heard arguing with Greg and

Jodie. For a moment or two Jay thought things were going to turn unpleasant, but then the three voices subsided. He heard Jodie say, '. . . just forget it, right?' and someone put another, quieter CD on. There was a sound like the front door opening and shutting, but he wasn't concentrating on that because Robyn was looking directly at him, her eyes intent and bitter. He thought she might say something, but abruptly she changed her mind, brushed past him and headed for the living room. Again Jay left it half a minute before going after her, and when he did, he found her standing in the middle of the room staring around with a lost look on her face. Kiran was not there.

'He went,' said Jodie. Her eyes were sympathetic, though she was careful to keep it from her voice. 'Said he needed an early night.'

'Oh.' Robyn nodded. 'Right.'

She started to scan the floor, as though she was looking for something. There was a lot of stuff lying around; CD covers, people's sandals . . . suddenly Robyn swooped and snatched up a sheet of paper, screwed into a ball, that lay half-hidden under a table. She started to smooth it out, then saw that Jay had noticed and shoved it into her bag instead.

'I think I'll get an early night, too,' she said to

Jodie. 'Thanks for the invite; it's been great.'

Jay started to open his mouth, but Jodie made a negating gesture at him. 'Leave it,' she whispered, then to Robyn: 'See you tomorrow?'

'Yeah,' said Robyn, dully. 'Probably.'

She went, more quietly than Kiran had done. Jay stood staring at the closed door. Jodie had moved away; he knew why she had shut him up, and it had been the sensible thing. But where Robyn was concerned, Jay was not always sensible.

He said the usual 'see you later's to whoever was in earshot, then slipped out of the door and down the first flight of steep, uneven stairs. The flat was at the top of a house in the old part of town, and there were three floors before you reached ground level. As usual no one had got round to renewing the stairway bulbs, so the only lighting was a greyish glow from the moon through the windows at each landing. When he was halfway down Jay heard the street door open and close, and quickened his own steps.

The street door led on to the maze of narrow lanes that climbed up from the harbour. The night was as hot outside as indoors and the sense of oppression stronger, if anything, especially with the buildings jumbling and crowding all around. A narrow alley between two houses gave a glimpse of the sea on the harbour side, and he was in time to see the shadow that was Robyn moving away through the gap.

He followed, and emerged on the harbour front. There were people about, visitors mainly, sitting at the outside tables of pubs and cafés or peering in at the windows of the art galleries and gift shops, most of which were lit overnight in the summer season. Robyn was twenty metres ahead; she paused at the edge of the pavement, then crossed the road to the harbour wall, where she leaned on the railing, head on folded arms, and stared down at the beach. Jay approached slowly. He thought she was unaware of him, but as he moved up to join her she turned her head.

'There was no need,' she said. 'I'm fine.'

'I'd had enough, too.' He rested his own arms on the railing beside her. Towards the horizon, the sea glinted like a knife under the moon. The tide was going out and hardly made a sound; but for a distant thump of live music, probably from one of the pubs, everything was oddly quiet.

'It's not even eleven,' Robyn said. 'Some Friday night.'

There was a long pause, during which a scooter

went noisily past along the road. Then Jay said, 'I saw the piece of paper, Robyn. You've been trying again, haven't you?'

She shrugged. 'Yeah. For all the good it did me.'

'Did you show it to Kiran?'

A nod.

'And . . . ?'

'The usual.' She knew what he wanted to ask, and with a sigh she took the screwed-up paper from her bag and gave it to him. 'He just keeps saying the same thing – that it's totally wrong.'

Carefully, Jay smoothed the crumpled paper out and studied it as best he could in the dimness. It was a sketch of a girl's face; a long, narrow face framed by dark hair. Not a particularly attractive face, and the expression Robyn had given her made it worse. Her eyes looked savage and her mouth was contorted into a shape almost like a snarl. There was something animal about it; spiteful, almost vicious.

He gave the sketch back to Robyn and gazed at the boats left stranded by the tide, hulls canted at precarious angles, mooring ropes trailing across the damp sand. The sea looked purple, with thin, white wavelets at its edge, and he thought about the other beach, the surfing beach on the far side of town, and a figure standing on a rock . . .

'I wish I'd seen her properly.' There was a note of helpless confusion in his voice.

Robyn laughed humourlessly. 'I just wish they'd *found* her. They probably never will now, of course. What is it they say? If a body's not washed up within three days, that's usually it.'

'Yeah. But even if—'

She cut across him. 'If they'd found her, you see, I might have been able to get a second look. You know: for identification.'

'Oh, for Christ's sake! It was bad enough seeing her drown!'

'I know!' Robyn's fingers clenched and flexed on the rail. 'But if I could just get it right, it might help Kiran get this – this *obsession* out of his head.' She turned to look at Jay, suddenly distressed. 'You know how he's been; the way he keeps on and on about seeing her face before we lost her. It's like she's haunting him, and I feel . . . I just feel that if I could draw her the way *he* saw her, it would . . . I don't know . . . help, somehow.'

Jay sighed. He wanted to say: yes, of course it would help, and if you keep trying you *will* get it right eventually and then everything will be fine. That was what Robyn wanted to hear.

And it's bullshit.

He said aloud, 'You can't exorcise it for him, Robyn. He's got to do it for himself.'

'I know that.' She looked at him, and the misery in her eyes made him feel like a complete traitor. 'You don't need to remind me. I know.'

'Sorry.' Jay waved one hand, a helpless gesture expressing nothing of any use. 'But . . . look, I know how it is with you and Kiran, but can't you see how selfish he's being? Sure, he's upset because he tried to rescue that girl and he failed. But we were *all* there. We *all* had the same experience. Putting you through this – it isn't fair!'

'I offered,' Robyn countered, simply.

Jay's anger was rising. 'Oh, yeah, you offered, and Kiran took, and he keeps on taking! It's typical of him; it'd–' He stopped as he realised his feelings were getting out of control, and got a grip on himself.

Robyn had turned away and was staring at the sea again. He knew she had stopped listening, blocking his words from her mind because they weren't what she wanted anyone to say to her.

He sighed. 'Sorry,' he said again. Then: 'There's no point in this, is there? No point hanging around here. Unless you want to go back to the party?'

'No. I'm going home.'

'Right. Mind if I walk back with you?'

She shrugged. 'Whatever.'

It wasn't quite a dismissal, so Jay squashed the sting of her indifference and went with her as she started to walk.

Robyn's house was half a mile away, on the far side of the harbour, where the old town gave way to the newer and more suburban residential area. They passed the lifeboat house, closed and in darkness, the slipway empty; both of them looked but neither spoke as they followed the road round. Then, abruptly, Robyn said, 'You know what the theory is, don't you?'

'What?' Jay was shaken out of his thoughts.

'About her. The girl.'

'Ah.' He hesitated. 'I'm . . . not sure.'

She flicked him a look that he couldn't work out. 'No one's been reported missing, have they? Local or tourist. So they think she was probably a dropout from somewhere up country, and she came down here to kill herself because it was a place where nobody knew her.' Her mouth twitched cynically. 'Nice of her.'

Jay sighed. 'Have you shown your sketches to anyone else?' he asked. 'You know; the police, or coastguards. Pictures are better than words – they could help identify her.'

She shook her head. 'What's the point? They're not accurate.'

That was Kiran speaking, he thought, and it made him want to argue. 'They're still better than nothing.'

'No, they're not,' Robyn countered flatly. 'It'd just confuse everything. Anyway,' she tossed her hair back, 'I've only got this one left. I burned all the others.' Suddenly she looked at him again, a strange, hard look. 'And I couldn't exactly show them that, could I?'

'Why not?'

'Because of her face. The expression I gave her.'

'But if—'

'Oh, come on, Jay, don't bullshit me! I made her ugly. I made her look—' She stopped, biting the last word back and unwilling to say it.

'What?' Jay said. 'What did you make her look?'

Muscles in Robyn's throat worked. Then: 'Evil,' she said. 'Well, I did, didn't I? You saw it; I know what you thought when you looked at the sketch. I made her look *evil.*'

But for the sound of their footsteps there was silence for several seconds. At last Jay said, 'If you did . . . you must have had a reason.'

He knew instantly that he had made a big mistake.

Robyn's face tightened and her eyes took on the hurt, introverted look he had seen in them so often since the drowning. In a changed voice, a voice that was suddenly distant and controlled, she said, 'Well, I didn't have a reason. I got it wrong, OK? So the drawing's useless, and talking about it's useless, and I just want to go home.' She met his stare. 'There's no need to come with me any further.'

There was nothing else he could do. Jay nodded, feeling the last of the argumentative spirit drain out of him. 'Right. But if you want to—'

'I don't. Thanks. I don't want anything. See you.'

She walked on, and Jay watched until she was out of sight before he turned and started slowly back towards the harbour. There, he stopped and gripped the rail of the harbour wall, tightening his fists until it hurt. *She didn't mean a word of that crap about not having a reason. She saw the girl's face, just like Kiran did, and she drew what she saw.*

That was the nub of it, the thing that disturbed him. Maybe Robyn's sketch wasn't physically accurate, not completely. But the *essence* of what she had drawn was right. He *was* certain of that.

So, he felt convinced, was Robyn.

Three

All in all, this has been a pretty shit day so far. Started off with a dose of complete paranoia about my GCSE results. I must have been dreaming about them, because I woke up totally convinced that I'm going to get the worst grades in human history. Even if it isn't true, I've still got weeks to go before I find out whether my whole future's gone down the tubes. That put me in a foul mood. Then I had a row with Mum about not getting any kind of summer job fixed up yet. I keep meaning to, but I've had other things on my mind. Anyway, I ended up feeling guilty, so I said, OK, I'll sort it, today, now. And it took me about ten seconds to find out that I've left it too late to get anything worth doing; all the decent work's been snapped up and there's only the crap stuff left. So now I'm faced with six weeks being a kitchen-help in a tourist restaurant. Great.

I didn't even feel like going to the beach after that, even though this has got to be the hottest afternoon so far this year. So there I am sitting outside the Blue Reef near the harbour, drowning my sorrows with a latte that cost a bomb, when Kiran shows up. Being with someone who's just about guaranteed to get an A in everything doesn't help right at this moment. And of course he organized his holiday job ages ago and, as you'd expect, it was the one everybody wanted – working at the surf shop on the beach.

Not that you'd know it, though. Because Kiran's mood is something else. He doesn't seem to give a toss about his results. In fact he doesn't seem to give much of a toss about anything at the moment. Like when I said he was a lucky sod to have landed that job . . .

Kiran stared across the street at the window of a souvenir shop and shrugged. 'It's nothing special. Just a job. You could have done it, if you'd got yourself sorted earlier.'

Jay looked down at his own feet, which had a coating of pavement dust over their summer brown. (Kiran's feet, he noticed, were browner.) 'I'd better warn Robyn,' he said, trying not to be needled by Kiran's careless tone. 'If she hasn't got anything yet—'

'She has. Helping out in some gallery somewhere in town.'

Jay's head came up. 'She didn't tell me.'

'Uh?' Kiran was still staring at the shop window and seemed to be having trouble concentrating. 'Didn't she? Well, there's no particular reason why she should, is there?'

No, there isn't. But she told you all about it, didn't she?

'I thought she might be around today,' Jay said diffidently, fishing. 'But I haven't seen her.'

'She's gone over to Falmouth.'

'Oh?'

'Yeah. Open day at the art college, or something; she's been on about it for weeks.'

Jay remembered. 'I didn't know it was today.' Nobody had told him that either, of course. He paused. 'I thought you were going to that with her?'

'Didn't feel like it.' Then suddenly Kiran's mind focused more sharply and he gave Jay a resentful glare. 'What is this, some kind of inquisition?'

'Of course it isn't!' Jay retorted defensively, then subsided. 'I just thought you'd go, that's all. We all know how keen she is on studying art after sixth form. It's the only thing she wants to do.'

Kiran shrugged again. 'She'll do it, then, won't she? You know Robyn.'

Jay's edginess abruptly spilled over into anger. 'Yes, she will – and I'm interested, even if you're not! What the hell's the matter with you, Kiran?' He laughed shortly and without humour. 'As if I hadn't worked it out.'

'If you have, then you don't need me to tell you, do you?' Kiran didn't – or wouldn't – meet his eyes.

'It's that girl,' Jay said flatly. 'The one who drowned. It's still bugging you, only you're so uptight you won't even *talk* to anyone about it.'

'What's the point?' Kiran countered. 'She died. I saw it happen. End of story.'

'We all saw it happen! Do you think it hasn't affected Robyn? Or me?'

Yet another shrug. Kiran wasn't going to be drawn.

'Look,' Jay said, making a last effort, 'I saw Robyn's sketches; the ones you got her to do—'

That did produce a reaction. Kiran's head came round and he said sharply, 'She wasn't meant to show them to anyone else.'

'Well, she did. That night after Greg and Jodie's party, I saw the latest one. Remember? The one you said was totally wrong?'

'It *was* wrong. They all are. Robyn thinks she can remember properly, but she can't.' Kiran's face contorted suddenly. 'Those sketches all make her look ugly. She wasn't. She was beautiful.'

It was a flat, matter-of-fact statement that didn't brook any contradiction. Nonetheless Jay wanted to contradict; in the circumstances, he had more faith in the accuracy of Robyn's memory than of Kiran's. But he looked at Kiran's face again, and the words would not come. *I haven't got the bottle to stand up for myself and really argue the toss with him.*

Abruptly, Kiran stood up. 'I'm going to the beach,' he said.

'The sea's flat.'

'Then I'll chill at the surf club.' He paused. 'Coming?'

Jay tried to think of a better option but couldn't. He sighed. 'OK. Might as well.'

They left the table and headed towards the nearest of the alleys that led to the surfing beach. Kiran didn't speak, and Jay could think of nothing worth saying. Even through flip-flops he could feel the heat in the pavement; the sun was so fierce that it made his arms and the back of his neck prickle. There was hardly a breath of wind, and the contrast between hard shadows and dazzling light made everything look faintly unreal.

They had turned into the alley and were walking up the steepening hill when Kiran suddenly stopped dead, staring. Jay followed the direction of his gaze. Several people were walking ahead of them. Other than that . . . Flower boxes in front of cottages, baker's on the next corner, a B&B with a No Vacancies sign, a white cat sunning itself on a sill. Shapes and colours dithered in the heat haze, but there was nothing remarkable that Jay could see.

'What is it?' he said.

Kiran didn't reply. He was still staring. Then, taking Jay by surprise, he moved again, striding away up the hill at an increasing pace until he was almost running.

'Kiran!' Jay went after him. At the top, the alley opened into a wider, crosswise street. Kiran disappeared round the corner; Jay followed, and found him some ten metres down the street, standing motionless in the middle of the road and looking like he had just slammed into a stone wall.

'Kiran, what's up with you?' A horn hooted behind them, and Jay pushed Kiran towards the pavement so that the car he had been blocking could pass.

Kiran said: 'It was her.'

'Who was who? What are you on about?'

'Her,' Kiran repeated, then swung to face Jay. His face had lost most of its colour and his eyes were dazed with shock. 'The girl. It was *her*!'

Jay had a horrible feeling that he knew what Kiran meant, and a sensation of dread clutched somewhere around the pit of his stomach.

'No,' he said. 'No, mate, *no*. It wasn't. It couldn't have been. Kiran, she's *dead*!'

'She's not,' Kiran contradicted flatly. 'I just saw

her.' Fury flared in his face and his voice rose to a shout. 'Do you think I wouldn't recognize her?'

Passers-by turned their heads curiously. 'Don't yell at me!' Jay hissed. Sweat trickled over his skin from the exertion of running. 'Look,' he went on, 'just think logically, all right? We know what happened to that girl. We were there. You said it yourself. She died. You *must* have made a mistake!'

Kiran's teeth were clenched. 'I did not!'

'OK. So where is she now?'

'I don't know!' Kiran's anger, which had ebbed, started to rise again. 'Why the hell do you think I'm standing here in the middle of the street? I came out of the alley and she'd *gone*. She's not here now, I didn't see which way she went, so I don't bloody *know*!'

'All right, all right!' Jay held up pacifying hands, palms outward. There was no point trying to reason with Kiran at the moment, so he scanned the street in both directions, looking for a hint of something familiar among the holiday crowd. *Back views of two girls with long, dark hair. One tanned, one pale. Both wearing beach gear. Could be anyone. But not her. It isn't possible. Whatever Kiran thinks, it isn't possible. And that's what scares me . . .*

'Come on,' he said to Kiran, trying to sound a lot

more confident than he felt. 'Maybe this isn't a good time to talk about it, yeah? Maybe when you've calmed down—'

Kiran turned such a savagely hostile look on him that he flinched. For a second or two their gazes held. Then Kiran said savagely, 'Go to hell!'

He stalked away, blindly it seemed, neither knowing nor caring where he was going but just determined to get away. Jay stared after him, confused. Part of him wanted to follow and resolve the situation; another part felt insulted and belittled and wouldn't have cared at that moment if Kiran had walked under a truck. The only certainty in his mind was that something was very wrong with Kiran. And he didn't know where to start putting it right.

Jay was at the stop when the Falmouth bus arrived and Robyn got off. Robyn didn't see him at first; she was fiddling with her mobile as she came down the bus steps, and only looked up when he called her name.

'Jay.' She was surprised. 'Hi. What are you doing here?'

'Thought I'd come and meet you.' And because he hadn't known which bus she would catch and so

39

had been waiting for more than two hours, he added, 'I've only just got here.'

'Oh. Right.' She looked around. 'Is Kiran with you? I was just going to call him.'

'He isn't here. And *I've* been trying to call *you*; only—'

'I know; I switched my mobile off. You know how people always ring when you're in the middle of something important; it's a real pain, isn't it?'

'Yeah.' Jay fell into step as she turned in the direction of her home. *Something important. Oh, yes. How the hell do I start?* He chickened out and said, 'How was the open day?'

Robyn's expression changed instantly. 'It was *brilliant*! The graduate show was on too – honestly, the standard's amazing. And the facilities – I've got to get in there, Jay. I don't care what it takes, I've *got* to! Kiran should have come. And you, too,' she added as an afterthought. 'You'd both have loved it. Look, I'll call Kiran now, and maybe we can all meet up at the beach café once I've been home for a shower, yeah?'

Get it over with. 'There's something you ought to know about,' said Jay. 'Now, I mean. Before you go anywhere.'

Robyn stopped walking and looked at him,

suddenly uneasy. 'What is it?' A pause, then her voice went up sharply. 'Is it Kiran? Has something happened?'

Jay nodded, then, as her unease started to turn to fear, he said hastily, 'Not an accident or anything; he's all right. At least . . .'

'*What*, for Christ's sake?'

So he told her. She listened without interrupting, and when he'd finished she sucked air in sharply through clamped teeth and stared down at the pavement.

'And you didn't see anything?' Her voice was outwardly level.

'No. Well, a couple of people who could have looked a bit like her from the back. But they weren't her. They couldn't have been, could they?'

'No . . .' Robyn was still holding her mobile; she made a move as if to use it, then changed her mind. 'Where's Kiran now?'

'I don't know. We were going to the beach, but . . .' The sentence tailed off.

'Right. So he could be anywhere.' She hesitated. 'I'll call him.'

Kiran's phone was switched off. Robyn did not leave a message but shoved her own mobile into her bag, blinked, and said, 'OK, he doesn't want to talk to anyone right now. I think we'd better look for him.'

'If that's what you want.'

'It is. I'll start with the beach. Coming?'

Jay sighed. He was beginning to wish he had never got into this.

'Yeah,' he said. 'Of course I am.'

The waves were small, and hardly anyone at the beach was making any attempt to surf, though there were enough holiday swimmers to keep the lifeguards alert. Robyn's sharp eyes picked out Kiran at the eastern end of the beach, near the uneven projection of the Finger rocks. In shorts and without a longboard, he was standing thigh-deep in the water, arms folded, not doing anything but simply staring out to sea as the tide creamed round his legs.

Robyn started to walk towards him. She said nothing to Jay, but he knew what she was going to do without the need for any explanation. He did not go with her but stood watching. Robyn waded into the sea. Kiran turned and saw her; they exchanged a few words, though they were too far away for Jay to hear what was said. Kiran shrugged and seemed about to move off, but Robyn laid a hand on his arm and he relented. They began to talk. Jay turned away.

Well, that's it. Whatever they're saying, it's pretty clear that they don't need anyone else around. OK; I suppose I've done my bit. Might as well go home.

He wondered if Robyn or Kiran would look round in a while and notice that he had gone. But he doubted it.

Four

If that had been the end of it – a one-off – then we'd all have let it blow over; even Kiran, with a bit of time. But that's the problem. It wasn't the end: it was just the beginning. And after nearly two weeks, I'm seriously worried.

Term's officially over now and I'm slogging at this lousy restaurant job most lunchtimes and evenings, which doesn't leave a lot of space for getting around. Kiran's working at the surf shop; or at least I suppose he is, though he never seems to be there when I go to the beach. Robyn says she's hardly seen him. She's pretty upset, because she knows he's giving her the runaround and she knows why. I still don't know what they said to each other that day when the first incident happened; she won't tell me. But things have moved on a lot since then. And the way they have moved is very disturbing. Which is why I virtually blackmailed Robyn into meeting me here after work today and made her promise not to say a word to Kiran . . .

Robyn was late. Jay had started to fear that she wouldn't turn up at all, but at last he saw her hurrying along the harbour front from the direction of the art gallery where she was working for the summer.

'Sorry.' She scraped out the chair opposite his at the pavement-café table and sat down. 'Last-minute customer who couldn't make his mind up what he wanted. Didn't buy anything in the end. Typical . . .' She saw Jay's face and her expression changed. 'So. What's this about?'

'You know what it's about,' Jay told her. 'Kiran, and that girl.' He leaned forward. 'Look, Robyn, this is getting out of hand.'

'Tell me about it.' Pain flickered in her eyes. 'Has it happened again?'

'Yes,' said Jay, flatly. 'Yesterday. And I was with him.'

A waitress came to the table at that moment and asked what they wanted. Robyn's face was a tight, blank mask and she didn't speak, so Jay ordered two Cokes and a bowl of chilli potato wedges. As he ordered, another part of his mind was running through the list of incidents, like fast-forwarding a video tape. Five – no, six times now, Kiran had been convinced that he'd seen the girl who drowned.

Always in the old part of town, always in a street packed with people, and never close enough to be sure. But Kiran *was* sure. And yesterday . . .

The waitress left. When she was out of earshot, Robyn said quietly, 'Did *you* see her? I mean, the person Kiran thought was her?'

'Sort of. It was in Fore Street; you know how crowded it gets at this time of year—'

'Yes, yes, I know! Just tell me what you saw!'

And that's the major problem. Because I'm not certain what, or who, I did see. And the more I think about it, the more the doubts are starting to creep in.

'There was a girl walking ahead of us,' Jay said aloud. 'Long, dark hair, same sort of build—'

'What was she wearing?'

'White shorts and a blue T-shirt. Oh, and bare feet.' He recalled that detail in particular for some unknown reason. 'Anyway, Kiran reacted the same way he did the first time. You know—'

'No, I don't,' Robyn interrupted, with a bitter edge. 'I've never been with him when he thinks he sees her, so I wouldn't know, would I?'

Jay flushed. 'Sorry. OK: he stopped and stared, then he took off after her. But by the time he caught up she'd disappeared, and he couldn't find her again.'

'He looked?'

'Yeah, he looked. He dragged me round town for nearly an hour before he gave up. He was in a real state by then; like he was having a panic attack or something.'

'But he didn't see her again.'

'No.'

Robyn nodded. 'So it's the same story, then. She's always far enough away so he can't just walk up and look at her, and when he tries to get nearer, she melts into the crowd and vanishes.' She raised her eyes to meet Jay's. 'It's obvious what he's doing, isn't it? He doesn't *want* to see her up close, because he knows subconsciously that if he did, she'd turn out to be someone else.' Her mouth twisted humourlessly. 'It's a good psychological trick.'

'That's what I thought. Yesterday, though . . .'

Jay didn't continue, and she prompted with agitation, 'What?'

A mental picture came back to Jay's mind. The girl had been no more than twenty metres away. Kiran had headed towards her, speeding up, leaving Jay behind. Then the girl had turned her head.

He said, 'I got a look at her face.'

There was an uneasy silence before Robyn said, 'And?'

'I don't know. I can't be sure. But . . . Look, have you still got that sketch?'

She frowned, then delved into her shoulder-bag. Wordlessly, she handed over the crumpled paper. Jay looked at the drawing.

The expression's totally different. Hair wilder, and maybe a bit longer. But in other ways the likeness is close. Too close to ignore.

Robyn said tensely, 'Are you telling me you think it *was* the same girl?'

'No, of course I'm not!' But then another memory returned. Further back in time: Kiran and the girl struggling in the sea, a glimpse of eyes, a mouth . . .

'It couldn't have been her, because we both know she's dead.' Jay looked up from the paper. 'But could it have been her twin sister?'

'Shit . . .' Robyn stared at the sketch as if it might suddenly come alive and attack her. For a few seconds she looked frightened. Then she seemed to collect herself and force some of the tension away.

'Right.' Her voice was controlled. 'Let's look at the possibilities, yes?' She started to count on her fingers. 'One: you only imagined that she looked like that girl.'

'Hold on, I—'

'OK, OK, I just said "possibilities". Personally, I

don't reckon you did imagine it.' Jay subsided and she continued, 'Two: she *did* look like that girl, and it was just bad luck. Coincidence.'

'Agreed.'

'Three: it wasn't her, but it *was* a relative – like you said, her sister or something. I mean, it could make sense; someone in the family coming down to look for her?'

Any family would surely have heard about the drowning by now, but . . .

'Right,' said Jay, cautiously.

'Four: it–'

'Christ, how many ideas have you come up with?'

Robyn gave him a hard look. 'Five, actually. Can I go on?'

He subsided again and made an acquiescing gesture. 'Sorry.'

'Four: it really was her, and she isn't dead. In which case there's something very weird going on. And five: it was her ghost.'

Jay's stomach lurched. 'You don't believe in ghosts?'

'Of course not! But if I *did*, then I'd have to say it was possible, wouldn't I? And that's what really bothers me, Jay. What if Kiran's thinking along those lines – that she's a ghost, and she's come back to haunt him?'

In the past I'd have laughed at that. We both would. Kiran's always been as rational as it's possible to get, and with about as much imagination as a brick. But since that day on the beach, his whole character has somehow changed. It's like he's become a different person and we don't know him any more. And suddenly I realized that I couldn't argue with Robyn's logic. Not the idea that Kiran's being haunted, but the idea that maybe he believes he is . . .

'Yeah,' Robyn said, reading Jay's face. 'You see where I'm coming from, don't you? Kiran's totally fixated with that girl. In the state he's in, absolutely anything could be going on in his mind. And I don't know what to do about it.' She blinked, and water droplets glittered on her eyelashes. 'I just don't know what to *do*!'

Robyn and I talked for a while longer, but we didn't really get anywhere. I wanted to ask if she'd meet up with me again later, but I didn't think she would; anyway, I'm working tonight. So that was it. Until, when I was clearing tables near the end of my shift at the restaurant, something occurred to me. I should have thought of it before; in fact I should have noticed yesterday, when Kiran went after that girl. It was late, but I went out the back and rang Robyn . . .

'All right, so she ran away,' Robyn said, dubiously.

'But wouldn't anyone, if they saw a total stranger coming at them the way Kiran did?'

'No,' said Jay. 'Any normal person would either think he was going to go past, in which case they'd get out of the way, or they'd think he was going to attack them, in which case they'd yell. But she didn't. She saw Kiran, and she did a runner.'

'What about the first time you were with him?'

'She'd gone by the time I caught up. But she must have run then, or I'd have seen her.'

'So what you're saying is, she was deliberately trying not to come face-to-face with him?'

'Exactly. And I want to know why.'

There was silence. Just as Jay was wondering if the mobile connection had gone down, Robyn said, slowly and deliberately, 'Then *I* want to know two things. Who the hell is she – and what the hell is she playing at?'

Jay couldn't answer either question, but before he could say so, someone shouted at him to get back to work or they'd all be here all night.

'Look, I've got to go,' he said hastily. 'I've got a day off tomorrow – I'll be on the beach in the afternoon. See you there?'

'I don't know yet.' Robyn sounded unhappy. 'Maybe.' And she cut the connection.

* * *

It was the nearest I'd get to a promise from her. As it happened, she did turn up. I saw her arrive and waved, thinking she'd come over. She saw me, I'm sure of it, but instead of heading in my direction she went into the surf shop. I'd put my head round the door earlier, so I could have told her Kiran wasn't there, and I expected her to come straight out again. When she didn't, I went over. And discovered that there had been some unexpected developments . . .

The surf shop was having a slack moment; apart from a couple of browsing holidaymakers the only people there were Robyn and Steve, the manager. Robyn looked round as Jay came in, and when she saw him she turned to Steve.

'Give it to Jay, why don't you? *He* doesn't let people down.'

There was bitterness in her voice. Jay looked quickly from one to the other and said, 'What's going on?'

Steve opened his mouth but Robyn beat him to it. 'Kiran's been sacked. So Steve's got a job going.' She blinked, then suddenly pushed past Jay and walked out of the shop.

Jay made as if to go after her, but Steve said, 'Leave her for a few minutes, I would. She's a bit upset.'

Jay hesitated. '*Have* you sacked Kiran?'

'Had to, mate. He didn't turn up three days running; no explanation, no nothing, and he'd switched his mobile off. I finally got hold of him this morning and told him that was it. I've got to have someone reliable.' He raised questioning eyebrows. 'You interested?'

'What? Oh – uh . . . yeah, I am.' With an effort Jay forced himself to concentrate, though his mind was trying to be somewhere else.

'OK, that's fine with me. Start tomorrow, nine-thirty?'

'Uh . . . yeah.' Staff came and went on a daily basis in the restaurant and no one worried about things like notice. 'Brilliant. Thanks.' Then he couldn't stop himself from adding, 'So Robyn was pretty hacked off?'

'Well, I think there was a bit more to it. But I didn't ask.'

'Right . . . Maybe I'll go and talk to her. You know; see if I can help.'

'Sure,' said Steve, with a conspiratorial grin. 'See you tomorrow, then. Nine-thirty. And don't be late!'

Jay found Robyn in her favourite spot among the tumbled rocks at the foot of the cliff, not doing anything but just sitting on her turquoise towel and staring at the sea. She looked round as he approached and said, 'Did you get the job?'

'Yes.' He scrambled over the last of the rocks and sat down beside her. 'Thanks for that.'

She shrugged. 'It's OK. Kiran screwed up, so that's his problem.'

'Is he around?'

Another shrug. 'How should I know? He doesn't bother to tell me anything.' Suddenly her face tightened. 'Like the fact that he's pulled out of the Brittany trip.'

'What?' Jay was nonplussed. A group from the surf club were taking a minibus to Brittany for ten days' camping. Kiran had been one of the first to book a place; Robyn, of course, had booked as soon as Kiran did – and they were scheduled to leave in a week's time.

Not quite sure if he could believe what he was hearing, Jay said, 'You mean, he's *cancelled*?'

Robyn nodded. 'I found out from Greg this morning. So I rang Kiran and asked him what's going on.' She pulled savagely at a loose thread on her towel. 'He just said he's changed his mind; not interested any more.' A pause. 'And we both know why.'

Jay couldn't think what to say. He felt for Robyn, but knew that at this moment her self-control was too fragile to deal with sympathy. Cancelling the French trip. It was *crazy*.

'You'll still go, won't you?' He had a sudden impulsive thought that maybe he could scrape the money together and take Kiran's place. But Robyn put paid to the idea.

'What's the point?' she said, morosely. 'I was only going because he was. I might as well pull out too, and spend the cash on something else.'

He sighed, and tried to summon the nerve to tell her that she shouldn't let Kiran dictate her life like this. Before he could speak, though, she went on.

'There's another reason, too. Why I don't want to go.'

'Oh?'

He waited, while Robyn stared down at her feet. At last she said, 'You'll laugh.'

'Try me.'

Another long pause, then: 'Kiran's started coming down here surfing at strange hours.'

Unsure where this was leading, Jay said cautiously, 'How do you know?'

'Greg again.' Her mouth twitched. 'If you want to know anything that goes on here, ask my brother.

He was shore fishing the other night and he saw Kiran.' She gave Jay a quick, defensive look. 'If you really want to know, I've followed him a couple of times since Greg told me. It's always the same; Kiran turns up after everyone else has gone for the day, and he stays in the sea till after dark. *Every* evening.'

'That's weird . . .'

She gave a cynical laugh. 'Weird? I'd call it bloody obsessive. I mean, what does he think it's going to achieve? Does he think she's suddenly going to leap out of the water and shout, "Hi, here I am, I'm not dead after all"?'

'No,' said Jay soberly. 'But try turning what you said around a bit. What if he thinks she might leap out of the water and tell him she *is* dead?'

Robyn's face became very still and a little grey under its tan. 'What do you mean?'

This wasn't going to be easy to say to her, but Jay felt he had to share the thoughts that were creeping into his mind. Because those thoughts frightened him.

'Yesterday, you said that Kiran might believe he's being haunted. All right. Let's say he *does* believe it. He thinks the girl is a ghost, and he's trying to make contact with her. Where's the most obvious place to look?'

Robyn's face was greyer. 'The place where she died . . .'

'Got it. So he comes here to look for her when there's no one else around.' Jay paused. 'Does he know you've followed him?'

She shook her head. 'I made sure he didn't see me.'

'And he didn't try to do anything . . . stupid?'

He was referring to the risks and dangers of the sea, and Robyn followed his track clearly. The muscles in her throat convulsed. 'No,' she said, then added, so quietly that the words were barely audible, 'Not yet, anyway.'

They regarded each other, both with the same ugly thought in mind. Neither spoke for several seconds. Behind them, the sound of the sea was a steady, relentless hiss and roar as the breakers rolled in.

Then Robyn said, 'It could happen, couldn't it? One mistake; accident or—'

'Deliberate. Yes.' *Say it. You've got to. It's only fair to Robyn and to yourself.* 'If Kiran's in as bad a way as we think he is, he could end up dead, too.'

Five

I had my doubts, but Robyn asked me to help her so, of course, I said yes. Carrying out surveillance is a bit of a strange experience. Forget all the spy movies; the first thing you find out is that it's boring, uncomfortable, and soon makes you want to forget the whole thing and go to sleep. But I didn't say that to her. Truthfully, I was worried enough about Kiran to go along with it and keep quiet.

Not that anything happened. We kept it up for the best part of a week; I did the morning watch and she took the late one. Just lurking on the beach, keeping an eye on Kiran. Crazy, really. All Kiran did was surf. Oh, yeah; and hang around the Finger sometimes, just standing there staring out to sea. I didn't see any ghosts, and I don't think he did, either.

But he did see me, on the sixth morning. My fault; I was dumb enough to get cramp in one leg and move at the wrong moment. Kiran didn't come over and challenge me or anything like that, and when I saw him in town later he didn't say a word about it. But I've told Robyn that's enough. He's sussed what we're doing, and if we carry on doing it, then whatever friendship either of us has got left with Kiran will be over, kaput, no right of appeal. At the very least, it's going to make him even more secretive than he already is. Robyn doesn't like it, but she sees I'm right. I think she still went down to the beach that night, though. But I didn't ask.

We've both tried to talk some sense into Kiran, but so far we've achieved absolutely zero. And we're starting to ask ourselves a few questions. In fact, we're starting to wonder if this girl Kiran's so obsessed with exists at all. Yeah, he's seen her – or someone who looks like her. But was it always the same girl? I'm seriously beginning to doubt it. Twice I was with him when it happened, but that doesn't prove anything. The first time, I didn't even set eyes on her. And the second time . . . well, her face was pretty similar to the one in Robyn's sketch, but so what? How many people in the world have lookalikes?

The thing that scares me is, if Kiran is mistaking various different girls for the one who drowned, then he's creating some kind of weird fantasy. I don't want to go over the top about this, but it's got to be faced: if something – or someone – doesn't break the pattern, he could get completely unhinged. Robyn agrees. But she's had another thought; not one of her original five but something new. She's wondering if someone – identity and motive unknown – is playing some kind of malicious game with

Kiran. I asked her, who and why? She didn't have an answer, but she's clinging to the idea. It doesn't make much sense to me. But maybe, for her, it's less frightening than the other options.

The surf club left for their Brittany trip last night. Robyn cancelled her booking. She offered her place to me, but I said no. Obvious reasons ... Anyway, I slept badly last night, and now I'm late for work and feeling knackered. If Kiran turns up at the beach today I might have one more try at getting through to him.

Not that it'll do any good.

Steve raised his eyebrows and reminded Jay that he was only paid for the time he spent at work, but the surf shop was busy enough for him to let it go at that. It was another blisteringly hot day and the shop entrance faced the wrong way to get any advantage from the light, offshore breeze, so by mid-morning the atmosphere was airless and sweaty. Kiran did not put in an appearance, and neither did Robyn.

At twelve-thirty Steve told Jay to take his lunch-break. 'You've been on another planet all morning, mate. Go and chill for an hour, OK? Then maybe I'll get some sense out of you this afternoon.'

It was said with a wry grin, and Jay smiled back a tacit apology. His longboard was in the surf clubhouse; maybe half an hour in the sea might help him shake off the feeling that his brain was stuffed with wet sand.

He kicked his flip-flops off and under the counter, left the shop and gratefully breathed fresher air. Then stopped as he saw Robyn.

She was over by the eastward cliffs, in her favoured place among the rocks. But there was no board, no bikini, no familiar turquoise towel. Just Robyn, hunched over, with her face hidden in her hands.

Jay went to her, pushing past idling beachgoers, treading (painfully, but he didn't notice) on a child's abandoned plastic spade, narrowly missing walking straight over someone's picnic. Approaching, he called Robyn's name, but she did not look up. As he reached her, he heard her crying.

'Robyn?' Ignoring mussels and barnacles that scoured his feet, he took the shortest route over the rocks to where she sat. 'What is it? What's happened?'

She raised her head then. Her face was blotched and her eyes puffy and nose running, but for the first time he could remember, she made no effort to hide her state.

'What is it?' Jay asked again.

She stared at him, and said two bleak words. 'Kiran's gone.'

Jay's stomach turned liquid. '*Gone?*'

'To Brittany.'

The liquid sensation was overtaken by such a lurch of relief that Jay felt as if someone had punched him. 'Christ, I thought you meant he was dead!' Then the implications caught up with him. 'Hang on – you mean, he's left with the others? On the minibus?'

She nodded dismally. 'I tried to ring him last night, and when I couldn't get his mobile I tried him at home. I talked to his mum. Apparently he changed his mind at the last minute. His place hadn't been taken by anyone else, so . . .' she shrugged, '. . . he went.'

'Just like that, without telling anyone?'

'He told his parents. Obviously.'

'Yes, but . . .' Jay ran out of words as a mixture of astonishment and anger got the better of him. 'I don't believe this!' he managed at last.

'Join the queue.'

'He knew you only cancelled your booking because you thought he wasn't going!' Jay sat down on the rock beside her. 'What's he playing at?'

'Leave it, Jay.' Robyn pushed the heel of one hand

across her face, trying to get rid of the tear streaks. Then she took a tissue from her shoulder-bag and blew her nose loudly. Sniffing, she went on, 'It doesn't take a genius to work it out, does it? It's Kiran's way of saying he wants me off his back. OK. Message understood.'

'Is that what you think?'

'Yes, I do. And don't start saying I'm wrong and try to be kind, or I'll throw something at you.'

'Oh, Robyn . . .' He reached out to touch her but she shrank away.

'Don't. I'm fine; I just want to be left alone for a bit.' She made herself look him in the face, though it clearly took an effort. 'I'll come into the shop later. Maybe we can get a bit of surfing in when you've finished work, if you're up for it?'

The careless tone, the matter-of-fact suggestion, was her way of dealing with her emotions and trying to overcome them. Understanding, Jay nodded. 'That'd be good.'

He wanted to stay, but Robyn had dropped too broad a hint for him not to take it. Before he'd even started to climb back over the rocks she was rummaging in her bag, and then, when he looked back he saw that she had produced a sketchbook and pencil. Glancing for the last time, he was left with an image of her crouched over the pad, taut with concentration.

He sighed, and walked slowly away.

Robyn came to the shop just before it closed. By that time, Jay had bored Steve nearly to distraction with his opinion of Kiran and what he had done. Steve was his usual phlegmatic self; Kiran, he said, was about as reliable as a paper wetsuit, and he couldn't see why Jay was so surprised and worked up about it.

'Anyway, why are you complaining?' he pointed out. 'Clears the field for you, doesn't it?'

Jay put that remark firmly out of his head as, with the shop locked up for the night, he and Robyn fetched their longboards from the clubhouse. There wasn't much surf, but what there was Robyn rode with a kind of ferocious energy that Jay had rarely, if ever, seen in her. She took several headers into the sea and collected a few bruises, but when at last they came ashore she seemed a lot calmer than when they had gone in.

'Good?' Jay asked, as they padded over the sand.

'Not bad.' It was non-committal but she managed a smile.

There was no one else around at the clubhouse;

Robyn claimed the shower before he could, so he sat on one of the benches while he waited for her to emerge.

Her bag was nearby and he could see the edge of her sketchbook poking out. *Shouldn't really do this, but . . .* He took the book and opened it. Last time he looked, the first few pages had been filled with quick drawings of Kiran surfing. These had now been torn out. And the next few sheets were sketches of someone else.

Jay felt cold suddenly as he looked at them. He recognized the face immediately; Robyn was too good an artist not to have caught the likeness. The drowned girl. But she had taken on a new and disturbing life, for Robyn had drawn her with a variety of different clothes, different poses, different expressions. It was as if the girl was one individual with a dozen personalities. Or as if Robyn was desperately trying to capture one trait, just one, that eluded her.

'You weren't supposed to see those.'

Jay started, and looked up to find Robyn standing in front of him.

'I'm sorry.' There was nothing else he could say.

She sighed. 'Oh, it doesn't matter. I didn't achieve what I wanted to, anyway.'

'Which was?' Jay began to suspect that his theory was right. But Robyn turned away so that he could no longer see her expression.

Towelling her hair, she said lightly, 'I don't know, really. Maybe I was looking for something I'd missed before. But if I was, I didn't find it. As Kiran would probably say, those are all crap. I'll chuck them when I get home.'

Jay looked at the sketches again and had a sudden, inexplicable urge. 'If you don't want them,' he said, 'can I have them?'

She looked at him over her shoulder, curious and a little suspicious. 'I suppose so,' she said at last, reluctantly. 'But don't show them to anyone else, all right?'

'Of course I won't.' Exactly what he would do with them Jay didn't yet know. But for some reason he thought they ought to be kept.

Robyn tore the sketches out of the book and dropped them on the bench. 'I'm going home,' she said, shaking her hair out. She stuffed the damp towel back into her bag and threw her wetsuit over her shoulder. 'Are you going to shower?'

'What? Oh – yes, I suppose so.'

'Well, I won't hang around and wait for you.' To take the edge off the remark she added, 'I'm working tomorrow and I'm pretty tired. See you later, yeah?'

She gave him no time to think anything else, let alone say it, but whisked out of the clubhouse almost at a run. For a few moments Jay stared at the empty doorway. Then he tucked the sketches carefully out of sight under his clothes and went to have his shower.

After a hot June and July, the weather in August was more often than not a let-down. This year, though, there were no signs of change. If anything the heat was increasing; Cornwall basked in long, cloudless days with light winds and climbing temperatures, and the town and beaches became more and more crowded as holiday visitors packed in. Along with just about everyone else, the surf shop was having its busiest year ever. Steve had increased Jay's hours after his first week – Jay grumbled about the lack of spare surfing time, but the extra money in his pocket was some compensation.

The Brittany campers had been gone for eight days. A few scribbled postcards had arrived at the surf club, but none of them was from Kiran, and when Jay met Robyn briefly on the beach she said that she hadn't heard from him either. Even his parents, she added, had heard nothing, which was about what she had expected.

Jay had expected it too . . . until Pogo came into the shop.

Pogo was a New Zealander, a keen surfer with one of the sunniest natures going. This morning though, he was, as Steve put it, not a happy bunny.

'I wouldn't have minded if there'd been two places up for grabs,' Jay overheard him complaining. 'But someone else had already taken Robyn's, and there was just Kiran's left. So she says, "Great, I'll have it, I'm off, see you in two weeks." I mean, I thought we were an item, right?'

Jay frowned and turned round, interrupting Steve as he started to agree with gloomy relish, 'That's women for you, mate.'

'Hang on – did you say *Kiran's* place?'

Pogo and Steve both stared at him. 'Yeah,' said Pogo. 'Nikki took it. You know? My girlfriend? Or I thought she was, anyway.'

'But Kiran went on the trip,' said Jay.

Pogo shook his head. 'Nah, man. He cancelled, remember? Just my luck.'

'Yeah, but he changed his mind again and went. Last minute. I know, because–'

'If Pogo says Nikki had Kiran's ticket, then she did.' Steve sounded irritated. 'What's with the inquisition all of a sudden?'

Jay took a grip on himself. 'Sorry . . . But look, are you sure it was his ticket she had?'

Pogo laughed. 'Sure. I saw the minibus off, man, and Kiran was *not* on it.'

A customer demanded Jay's attention then, and by the time he'd finished sorting out a boogie-board hire, Pogo had gone. Steve wanted to know what Jay had been getting so worked up about, but Jay avoided answering. Inwardly, though, he was thinking hard – and starting to worry in a big way.

If Pogo says Nikki had Kiran's ticket, then she did. Kiran had not gone to Brittany. His parents thought he was there; Robyn thought he was there. But he wasn't. So where the hell *was* he?

The obvious thing, and the thing Jay didn't want to face, was that there was a connection with the mysterious girl. Had to be; Kiran's growing obsession since the drowning was the only possible reason for him to have lied to everyone who mattered and gone off, God alone knew where, on his own. That suggested – though Jay didn't like the thought – that there had been some kind of development, and Kiran wanted to follow it up

69

without anyone else finding out. It was hard to imagine what it could possibly be.

Telling Robyn was going to be harder still.

Robyn's eyes were over-bright as she stared at Jay with a mixture of shock and fear. 'Something's wrong,' she said in an unsteady voice. 'I know it is. I just *know*.'

'Yeah,' Jay agreed. 'But what?'

She shook her head so hard that her hair whipped stingingly across her face. 'That's not the point! Trying to second-guess Kiran's a waste of time – whatever it is, we've got to do something about it.' She looked at him again. 'I think he's in danger.'

'What from?'

'From *himself*!' She was sounding shrill now. 'What d'you think I meant? He's losing it, Jay; he's been losing it for weeks! If he's gone somewhere trying to find this girl – whatever he thinks she is – then the state he's in, he could end up doing something stupid!'

She didn't need to elaborate. Jay understood and, even if he did not necessarily agree with her, the situation couldn't be left to sort itself out.

'What do you think we should do?' he asked.

'We can start by searching all the local coast and

beaches,' she said firmly. 'Because I'll tell you one thing – wherever he is, he won't be far from the sea.'

That made sense. 'What about his mobile?' Jay asked.

She gave him a pitying glare. 'He's got it switched on and he's going to answer? I don't think so.'

'OK, OK!' Jay held up placating hands. 'It was just a thought.'

'Well, it was a dumb one. What time do you finish at the shop?'

'Six-thirty. That's if Steve doesn't make me stay behind and scrub the floor or something, for overstaying my lunch-break.' He glanced at his watch. 'I'm already twenty minutes late back.'

Robyn ignored that. 'Six-thirty, then. I'll meet you outside and we'll get started.'

He didn't argue. When Robyn got the bit between her teeth, there was no point. And anyway, he didn't want to argue with her. He never did.

Six

We searched until it was just about too dark to see where we were going. Even then, Robyn wanted to carry on, but I put my foot down and made her give up. It was a weird feeling, being that tough with her; I've never had the nerve to do it before. But she didn't even argue. Something inside her just sort of collapsed, and suddenly she seemed vulnerable and helpless. She wouldn't admit it, of course, but I think she desperately wanted someone – even me – to tell her what to do, because she didn't know any more.

That was the first day. We covered a fair bit of ground in the limited time we had; the three main town beaches, plus the harbour. Neither of us really expected to find Kiran, of course – if he was holed up around any of those places, someone would have seen him and we'd have known about it before now. But it made Robyn feel that at least we were trying.

The second day – yesterday – was a bit better organized. Steve didn't like it, but I texted everyone I could think of who might know anything. I was subtle about it, as Robyn doesn't want anyone else to know what's happened. (I don't know why, but it's her choice.) Didn't get any replies. Then she took the afternoon off work and went round the cafés and places like that to see if he'd turned up lately. Again, nothing. In the evening we went out again, just looking. Zilch.

Now though, it's the third day, early evening, and Robyn's just called. She's at her brother's flat, and she wants me to meet her there. Wouldn't say what it's about but . . . I don't know; she sounded really strange . . .

Greg and Jodie weren't at the flat when Jay arrived. Robyn answered the door buzzer, and when he reached the top of the stairs she was waiting. She seemed jumpy, her movements quick and restless as though there was something she couldn't wait to tell him.

Outside the sun was still bright, but Robyn had closed the curtains over all the flat's windows. One candle stuck to a saucer burned in the living room, making it look and feel stifling, and bringing back memories of the party a few weeks ago. Robyn had littered the floor with sheets of paper, and every sheet was covered with rough, almost scribbled drawings. Jay presumed they were hers. But they were nothing like her usual style.

'Jay, something weird's happened.' She didn't

offer him coffee or anything, but dropped to her knees beside the scattered pages. 'Look at these, just look!'

He took the random handful she thrust at him and frowned. 'Did you do them?'

'Yes, and they don't look anything like my normal stuff, do they? That's the point.' She raised her eyes to meet his. Her gaze was very intense. 'Do you know about automatic writing?'

'Sure – it's like a ouija board, only it's done with a pencil and paper. Messages are supposed to come through, and . . .' The explanation faded as he began to understand.

'That's it,' said Robyn. 'That's what's happened. Only it isn't writing, it's *drawing*.'

It was pretty straightforward, really. Robyn had been in her room at home, trying to sketch the girl again, when she found that – well, as she put it, 'the pencil took over.' Next thing she knew, she'd produced some really bizarre pictures that didn't make any sense. They've just got two things in common: one, she can't remember doing them, and two, every one has that girl's face in it somewhere.

'I tried again,' she said, 'but my mood must have changed or something, because it didn't work any more. I thought maybe I couldn't concentrate because Mum and Dad were around, so I asked Greg if I could come here, because I knew he and Jodie were going out.'

'And?'

'Nothing. It didn't come through. So then I thought—'

'Hold on,' he said. 'What do you mean, "come through"? You're not saying it's some kind of message from the other side?'

'No! I'm talking about my *subconscious*. We don't know *anything* about the human mind, what it's capable of! Look at those psychics who find missing people with a pendulum and a map!'

'I've heard the stories, but—'

'They're *true*! They're on police records, even if the police don't like admitting it! The subconscious is incredible; we can sense things, understand things, know things—'

'Like where Kiran is?'

'Why not?' There was a wild challenge in her voice and in her look. 'What have we got to lose by trying?'

'We?'

'Listen, Jay – I *did* this, but now it won't come back again, and I think it's because I haven't got the – the *energy* any more, not on my own. But if *two* of us try, that doubles the odds, doesn't it?'

Jay knew then that he wasn't going to talk her out of this. She was tense, sparking, ready to get what she wanted by any means she could.

'OK,' he said. 'What do you want me to do?'

'Shut your eyes,' Robyn said sharply.

He obeyed, wanting to sigh but stopping himself in time. The flat was very hot, and the pencil felt sticky in his fingers. The only pleasurable part of it – *which is about as pathetic as it's possible to get* – was that Robyn's hand was on the pencil too, and so touching his. He couldn't see his watch, so didn't know how long they had been sitting like this, cross-legged, with the pencil poised over a large sheet of paper, but it felt like about a week. And nothing had happened. No chills down the spine, no sense of a looming presence, no sudden and violent movement as the pencil began to move of its own accord. *Some ghost movie.*

In the distance a car alarm went off. Jay's efforts to concentrate collapsed and he opened his eyes again. *This is getting ridiculous. How much longer does she expect us to sit here? I haven't eaten yet, and I could murder a long, cold drink.*

But then he felt the pencil twitch. It surprised him, and instinctively he took a tighter grip.

'Don't!' Robyn hissed. 'Let it go; let it do what it wants!'

Her own fingers were loose on the pencil's shaft – and now the pencil really was moving. It touched the paper, skidded across it, dug a small tear. Then suddenly it started to dash over the page in a random scrawl. Lines appeared. (A star? No, it was more like a tree; or maybe a fountain . . .) Jay stared with a kind of mesmerized incomprehension as the picture grew, apparently under its own momentum.

Robyn whispered tautly, 'It's coming through!'

For a moment Jay almost believed it, too . . . until his brain started to interpret what his eyes were seeing. What was 'coming through' was nothing but a meaningless scribble. There was no face, no coherent picture, nothing recognizable at all. OK, maybe their subconscious minds *were* directing the pencil. But it looked as if their subconscious minds didn't have a lot to say.

That's it. I've had enough. He felt sorry for Robyn, but she was doing herself no good with all this. Echoes of Kiran's obsession, almost: he should stop it, now, before she got so carried away that he couldn't get her back down to earth.

Jay drew breath to say all that and more, and was about to take his fingers from the pencil. But Robyn beat him to it. Abruptly, fiercely, she snapped, '*Let go!*' and batted his hand aside. Clutching the pencil, she crouched forward, hair falling over her face, shoulders hunched and her entire body radiating tense concentration. The pencil was still moving, but she was in control. And now something *was* taking form. Forgetting food, cold drinks and everything else, Jay watched as she drew. Her hand was rapid and confident, though her eyes were closed and she seemed to have no conscious knowledge of what she was doing. One sheet of paper was covered with sketches; she brushed it aside, started on a second, then on a third.

When she finally stopped, it was with a jolt that broke the pencil point. The pencil fell from her grasp, there was a long silence, then she let out a breath that shivered through the hot room, and opened her eyes.

'What did I draw?' The hectic excitement was gone and her voice was calm, almost dull.

Jay picked up the nearest sheet of paper. The sketch showed someone on a surfboard who might or might not be Kiran, and the style was very definitely Robyn's own. He set it aside, looked at the next sheet. This was covered with drawings of a girl's angry face, and Jay only needed one glance to recognize her. He reached for the last sheet, but Robyn was already looking at it. She stared, then passed it to him.

'What do you make of this?'

Unusually for her, it was a landscape sketch. A small, part-rocky and part-sandy cove, edged by low but steep cliffs and with a path winding down to the beach from the top.

'It sort of looks familiar . . .' Jay said.

'I know where it is.' Robyn was emphatic. 'It's that little cove just the other side of Clodgy Point.'

He peered. 'You sure?'

'Certain. It's pretty isolated; the tourists don't use it because the path down's tricky. And there's not much space for surfing; too many rocks.' She met his gaze. 'In other words, it's a pretty ideal place for someone who wants to get lost.'

Jay whistled softly. 'You think Kiran might be there?'

'I'd take bets on it.'

Jay didn't know, and didn't really want to know, how or why Robyn's mind had driven her to draw this particular location. *But it's a possibility. And as we don't have any better ideas at the moment, why not follow it up?*

'It's my day off tomorrow,' he told her. 'If you can

get out of work, we could go there in the morning—'

'Sod that.' In a single movement she swept up the papers into an untidy bunch and dumped them on the sofa. 'I'm going *now*.'

'What? Robyn, it's going to be dark in another hour!'

'Balls. The sky stays light till gone ten.' She had blown out the candle and was hacking the curtains open. Light streamed in, as if to back up what she was saying. 'You can come with me or stay; it's your choice. But I'm going.'

'Robyn, listen—'

She interrupted, swinging round to face him. 'Sorry, Jay. But I'm *doing* it! If you don't want to, then you'd better go home, because I can't leave you alone in Greg and Jodie's flat.' She shrugged. 'Well?'

Jay sighed. 'OK, then. I just hope there's a torch or something here that we can borrow.'

There were still plenty of people on the main beach and two separate barbecues were going on, one with what sounded like some pretty good music. But Robyn was oblivious to it all as she strode along the road towards the beach's westerly end, where the coast path began. Jay, following, was starting to feel as if he had been caught up in a surrealist movie. To their left the futuristic lines of the art gallery were rose-tinted by the evening light; the car park behind it, he noticed, was full.

Not looking where he was going, he tangled with a walking family group, and by the time he had apologized and extricated himself, Robyn was well ahead.

'Slow down, will you?' he called after her.

She stopped and waited impatiently for him to catch up. 'You were the one worrying about the daylight,' she reminded him. 'Come on!'

The beach fell behind them; past another, smaller car park and they were on the coastal path, which curved away around the low headland. Soon the only sound they could hear was the hiss of the sea, broken occasionally by a faint roar as a larger wave broke on the rocks below them. Again, there was hardly a breath of wind tonight; the scent of gorse was heavy in the air, mingling with the fresher brine smell. The sun was in Jay's eyes, making him blink; Robyn, though, hardly seemed to notice. She was walking faster, almost jogging; Jay concentrated on the ground under his feet, wishing he had something more sensible on than his usual flip-flops.

The cove was a little over a mile from the town,

and at the pace Robyn set it wasn't long before they saw the cleft of it, like a fold in dark velvet. They walked another couple of hundred meters or so, then Robyn turned off the main path and headed along a narrower and more overgrown track towards the beach.

The tide was halfway out, and the angle of the sun turned the water to a mercury-silver glitter. As the beach track turned downwards, something caught Jay's attention. He paused, shading his eyes. Something in the sea . . . A seal, maybe? Or was it just a half-submerged rock?

It was neither.

'Robyn!' His call brought her up short and he pointed. 'Someone's swimming down there.'

She followed his direction and drew in a sharp breath as she, too, saw the figure in the water. Jay knew what she was thinking and for a few moments he thought it, too. Kiran. *Could* it be?

Robyn said sharply, 'Come on!' and would have set off on the path again but Jay caught her arm, stopping her.

'Hold on a minute . . .' He had narrowed his gaze and was peering harder against the glare. Robyn hesitated, then looked too.

The swimming figure was coming out of the sea.

It emerged from a breaking wave, stood up in thigh-deep water, and Jay suddenly had serious doubts about his first assumptions. Whoever it was had long, dark hair, tied back the way Kiran often tied his. But a lot of other things were wrong. The stance, the movement: they weren't familiar. The build looked wrong, too: slighter, smaller than Kiran. From this distance and with the light so difficult, any certainties were out of the question. That shape could be anyone.

In fact, it could even be female . . .

Robyn said, 'It isn't him.'

The words were emphatic; even if Jay couldn't be sure, she was. He glanced at her. 'So who is it?'

'I don't know.' Her mouth set in a hard, tight line. 'Let's find out.'

She ran on down the path, and Jay went after her.

They took a few risks on the steep descent, but even so it was several minutes before they reached the sand. When they did, there was no one in sight.

'He's gone!' Robyn said, in dismay. 'We should have kept watching as we came down!'

'And broken our necks because we weren't looking where we going? Don't be crazy.'

She ignored that and scanned the sea, but no dark

head broke the water. 'How the hell did he *do* it? There was nowhere to go! No path on the other side, and he couldn't have come this way or we'd have seen him.'

'Or her,' said Jay.

She gave him a peculiar, searching look. '*Her?*'

Jay shrugged. 'I couldn't be sure, but . . . I thought it might be a woman.'

He could see Robyn considering that, though her inner reaction was impossible to judge. At last she uttered a sharp laugh, without humour.

'I suppose so,' she said. 'Really, it could have been anyone, couldn't it? A bloody mermaid, for all we know.'

'A merrow,' said Jay.

'What?'

I don't know why I said that. It just came out, without my wanting it to. But it had been lurking around in the back of my mind. Something I read or heard somewhere; a word, an idea. I should have kept it to myself. But it's too late now.

'It's another term for a mermaid,' he said, uncomfortably. 'Irish, I think. Merrow.' He looked down at his feet. 'I know it sounds totally crazy, but . . . There are legends, superstitions – you know the sort of thing. About merrows latching on to a particular human being and . . . kind of luring them, snaring them . . .'

I can feel the words collapsing. Robyn's staring at me as if I'm totally barking mad, and I don't blame her. Mermaids and legends – it's even more off the wall than the haunting theory. Why can't I learn to keep my mouth shut?

But in spite of the expression on her face, Robyn wasn't mocking him. For a few moments she went on staring. Then at length she said, quite quietly, 'Kiran's merrow. You're right; it is totally crazy. But in another way, it sort of fits, doesn't it?' Her shoulders hunched. 'I don't know where the hell you got that from, Jay, but maybe you've just summed up what's going on in his mind.'

'Have I? How?'

She shook her head. 'I don't want to start analysing it now. This isn't the time or the place; we've got something more important to do. Like finding out who that was in the sea, and where they've gone.' She turned slowly on one heel, her gaze raking across the beach. 'No sign of anyone. Not even any footprints, except ours . . . This is weird. You know what, I could almost start believing in merrows.'

It was an attempt to lighten the mood, but it didn't

work for either of them. Jay studied their surroundings again. There were a few small caves here, not to mention the tumbled rocks. Unlikely, but . . . 'Let's check the beach out. You never know.'

She nodded. 'OK. I suppose it's all we can do now.'

Jay was emerging from the last and smallest of the caves when he heard Robyn shout. She was on the other side of the beach, climbing among the rocks near the tideline, and she had something in her hand which she was waving at him. He broke into a run and reached her as she jumped down on to the sand.

'What have you found?'

'This.' She dropped a small object into his hand. A decorative leather-and-bead wristband. 'It was stuck between two rocks but I managed to get it out.' He realized that she was shaking, and then she added, 'It's Kiran's.'

A cold sensation washed over Jay's skin. 'Are you sure? How do you know?'

'Because I made it for him. So there isn't another one exactly like it in the world.'

Seven

The wristband proves that Kiran has been at the cove. I did wonder for a moment if maybe he could have lost the band in the sea nearer home and it washed up here, but that's stretching coincidence too far. Besides, the prevailing current would have carried it up coast, not down. No: he's been around here somewhere, and recently.

Could it have been him in the sea? The light was dazzling, and it was impossible to make out enough detail to be sure of anything. But Robyn and I both saw someone. So where are they now? The only thing either of us can think of is that they must have swum round the headland and gone ashore at the next cove along. There's a bigger beach round there, and it's not too difficult a swim for anyone who knows what they're doing.

Then Robyn remembered the holiday campsite behind the larger beach, a few hundred metres inland. It's nothing special; three or four fields with an ugly-looking shower block and admin building; but it's quite popular at this time of year. Maybe the swimmer came from there?

There's no point discussing what to do. I know Robyn's

going straight to the campsite, and she knows I'll come with her because I wouldn't get anywhere by arguing about it. She won't admit it, but I also think I know exactly what's going on in her mind.

She's put together all the pieces of evidence we've gathered so far, and to her they add up to one thing. Kiran is obsessed with a girl, but she isn't the girl who drowned. Kiran's merrow is as alive as any of us, and he's been seeing her behind Robyn's back.

It's the only explanation that makes any sense.

The sun had disappeared below the horizon by the time they reached the campsite, and dusk was not long away. The site was crowded; caravans and tents lined the fields, and lights shone in the shower block. A dog was barking somewhere, an incessant and irritating *yap, yap, yap* that set Jay's teeth on edge.

Robyn climbed over the stone hedge at the edge of the nearest field and stood staring around.

'Light's going,' Jay said. 'It'll be impossible to recognize anyone in a few minutes.'

She didn't answer, but started to walk across the fields. About half the caravans had lit windows – a lot of campers would probably have gone to restaurants in town – and light spilled through the opened flaps of some of the tents. Robyn walked on, looking left and right, now and then stopping to peer harder at something before moving on. A middle-aged couple, passing them, said, 'Evening'; Robyn ignored them and Jay mumbled a vague reply. A gate led to the second field, and again Robyn walked and looked and paused and moved on. The third field was the last and furthest from the facilities. There were no caravans here, only tents; the daylight really was failing now and in the increasing gloom the tents looked like oversized, strangely-shaped animals lying in the grass.

Then Robyn stopped again. She said nothing, but her body tensed and her gaze was fixed on something at the field's edge.

Jay looked. There was one tent against the hedge, a green, two-man dome type that would be easy to miss against the camouflaging background. A wetsuit was draped over it, partly covering a large, yellow patch where the tent had been repaired at some time in the past. The patch made the tent unmistakable. It was Kiran's.

The dog stopped yapping, and in the sudden quiet Jay could hear Robyn's quick breathing. He touched her arm to get her attention; she jumped, then looked round.

'Looks as if we've found him,' Jay whispered.

Still Robyn said nothing. She started to walk towards the tent.

'Robyn, what are you going to—'

'Shh!' She put a finger to her lips, soft-footed now as she approached the tent. Silent, Jay followed.

There was a light inside, dimly visible through the fabric. As they drew closer, they could hear murmuring. It was Kiran's voice, Jay was sure; impossible to make out any clear words, but from his tone it sounded as if he was talking to someone. Then he laughed, a peculiar, forced laugh. And the laugh was followed by another – higher-pitched, and female.

Robyn froze, and even in the gloom Jay could see the look of bitter shock on her face. *She knew the truth deep down, but she tried to convince herself she was wrong. Now though, she can't pretend any more . . .*

For two or three seconds, Robyn stood motionless. Then she turned and ran back across the field towards the gate.

Jay hesitated. Fury had hit him in a rush, bringing with it an urge to rip open the tent flap, burst in on Kiran and whoever was with him and tell them both exactly what he thought of them. But Robyn's reaction was a stronger pull. She had almost disappeared in the dusk; another few moments and he'd lose her altogether.

He ran after her, just managing to keep her in sight as she retraced her steps through the campsite, over the stone hedge and away along the coast path. By the time Jay reached the hedge he could no longer see her. But he had a good idea of where she was going, and when he reached the point where the track forked to the small cove, he saw her below him on the sand. He slithered down the path and finally caught up with her. She was standing at the sea's edge crying her heart out, and it took all Jay's willpower not to put his arms around her and hug her to him – or try.

She knew he was beside her, and suddenly her voice broke out in a cracked whisper. 'Bastard, bastard, bastard, *bastard*...' The words were muffled by tears and pain, but the rage Jay might have expected wasn't there. She simply sounded broken.

'I'm sorry.' What else could anyone say to her? Jay felt utterly helpless. At this moment he could have killed Kiran.

The edge of an incoming wave soaked Robyn's trainers but she didn't seem to notice. She wasn't sobbing now. There were just the tears, falling and falling as if they would never stop. And Jay's willpower deserted him. He moved closer and his arms went around her shoulders, drawing her close until her face was hidden against his chest and the bright crown of her hair touched and tickled his throat.

'Robyn . . .' He kissed her hair, stroked it, held her so tightly that he felt as if he would never be able to draw a breath again. He expected an angry rejection, because he was not Kiran, and it was Kiran who had hurt her and she wanted the hurt to stop and for everything to be all right again. But instead she was clinging to him, her body pressing and her fingers digging painfully into his back. He could feel the sharp spasms of her breathing as she tried to get herself under control. But he knew, too, that a part of her wanted to lose control altogether and hit back at Kiran in the only way she could.

Which is what I want, too. But for my reasons, not for hers. I wish I had the courage to take the step, make the move. I wish I could – but I can't, because even though Kiran isn't here, I can feel his influence like a ghost between us. I wish he'd been born on the other side of the world, and neither of us had ever met him.

Robyn's tears had dampened Jay's shoulder and upper arm, but now at last they were stopping. Her breathing eased, slowed a little. Then, abruptly, she pulled away from him and turned her back, walking a few unsteady paces away. He heard her sniff. Then she said quietly, 'I think I want to go home.'

'I'll take you.' His gaze didn't leave her for a moment.

She nodded, sniffed again. 'Yeah. Not much point staying around here, is there?'

He tried not to take that personally, though it was difficult. They walked back to the cliff path in silence. Then, as they began to climb, Robyn suddenly said, 'I've made a total idiot of myself, haven't I?'

Thinking she was referring to what had just taken place between them, he answered firmly, 'Of course not! Robyn, you know that I—'

She interrupted. 'Oh, yes I have. I should have seen it. I should have *known*. All that crap Kiran's been giving out about the girl who drowned. It's all lies; he made it up so I wouldn't realize what's *really* going on. He's got someone else.' She scrambled over an awkward patch in the path. 'So what does he do?' The pitch of her voice started to rise. 'He hasn't got the guts to tell the truth, so he frightens the life out of me by going off without a word, lying to me about it, leaving me to find out for myself that he'd gone missing – he could have been *dead* for all I knew!'

Jay did not answer. He was thinking that if anyone had been an idiot, it was him. Robyn's whole focus was still on Kiran. She wasn't thinking about their private moment; if she hadn't already forgotten it, it meant nothing to her. They climbed on, and neither said anything more until they reached the top of the cliff. Then Robyn spoke again, sounding calmer and more thoughtful. 'Or maybe the girl who drowned did have something to do with it. I mean, he was pretty devastated about not being able to save her, wasn't he?'

'We all were.'

She ignored that. 'Maybe it *did* get to him so badly that he started imagining he saw her around town. And then he met this – this other girl, and maybe . . . I don't know; maybe she looked a bit like the one who died.' She gave Jay a quick, pleading look. 'That time you were with him and saw her; you said she looked like my sketches . . . So maybe that's what got to Kiran. She's like a – a substitute. Maybe that's it.'

I've given up counting the 'maybes' and I wish I could agree with her. But I can't. What I think is that Kiran's behaved like a total shit, end of story. He's seeing someone

*else, but he doesn't want to be honest about it and split
with Robyn. He'd rather keep playing her along, keep her
as a standby in case the new relationship goes wrong.*

Robyn was waiting for Jay to reply, hoping that he
would back her up. But Jay couldn't do it and he
looked away unhappily.

'OK,' Robyn said quietly, after a few seconds. 'I
get the message. Switch the torch on, will you? I
can't see where I'm going.'

She set off, not waiting for him. Jay took the small
flashlight from his jeans pocket and fumbled in the
dimness for the on-switch. The light flicked on, and
as he started to follow Robyn he looked down to the
cove one last time.

The moon wasn't up yet, but a little light still
reflected from the western sky. The sea had a faint,
phosphorescent gleam . . . and a few metres out, he
saw what looked like someone swimming towards
the shore.

Quickly, he glanced along the path. Robyn was
some way ahead, her figure no more than a vague
silhouette. Should he tell her?

*Tell her what? That there's someone down there again?
What good would that do?*

Kiran's merrow . . . He resisted the urge to look at
the sea again, and went after her.

* * *

Robyn didn't say anything else all the way back, and neither did I. But as we walked, I started to get angry, and by the time the town lights came in sight the anger was so strong that I felt sick.

Robyn called herself an idiot. But I'm a far bigger prat, because Kiran conned me, too. For a while I nearly believed that there was something weird going on; especially that business of the girl in town running away whenever she saw Kiran. Correction – why she ran away when I was with Kiran. Because we've only got his word about the other times. I'd take bets that she only did a runner when she saw me, because she knows about Robyn and didn't want to risk someone working out the truth and blabbing it. Chances are Kiran primed her to do it, just in case.

Back at the cove I wanted to kill Kiran. Not now, of course; it was a heat of the moment thing. But this anger is getting to me. I don't want Kiran to get away with what he's done. I want it sorted, once and for all. I want to help Robyn, even if it's just by being around and trying to pick up the shattered bits of her illusions. The time isn't right, not yet; I learned that much on the beach. But I need to do something. And I can't stop thinking about that last glimpse I had of someone in the sea . . .

* * *

Jay offered to walk Robyn home but she said no. They parted company at the harbour; she didn't resist when he hugged her again, but she was passive, uninterested. Disengaging herself from him as soon as she could, she said, ''Night, then. Thanks for coming with me. I'll call you sometime.'

'Any time.' *But you already know that.* ''Night.'

He watched her go, and kept watching until she was out of sight. He didn't want to go home yet. He wanted time to think, and the down-to-earth atmosphere of home would be too distracting. The nauseous feeling had gone, and his anger had dulled to a sense of tight discomfort, like mild indigestion. On the walk back, he had come up with the idea of saying goodnight to Robyn and then going back to the campsite, where he would confront Kiran and tell him that he knew exactly what was going on. What that might lead to was something he hadn't yet thought through. But now, he was starting to modify the plan. *That last glimpse. Kiran's merrow.* He was right not to have told Robyn what he had seen. He didn't want to involve her in his newest thoughts, not yet. But he wanted some answers. And he wouldn't get them by leaving the questions until tomorrow.

Robyn would be almost home by now. It was gone

eleven, and people were starting to emerge on to the streets from the two pubs along the harbour front. The night felt hot, and the faint murmur of the low tide beyond the harbour wall had a peculiar, almost ominous tinge to it. Jay straightened up from the rail where he had been leaning, looked around. He saw a few of his friends among a small crowd not far away, but they had not noticed him and would be easy enough to avoid.

He turned, and began to walk quickly in the direction of his own house.

Eight

Walking in the dark, empty street, I keep telling myself that this is completely and utterly dumb, and the only sensible thing to do is turn round and go back home. I could get back into the house the same way I came out; through the bathroom window and on to the back extension roof, then it's only a two-metre drop into the back garden. Easy. Mum and Dad think I'm in bed; Dad's crashed out, too, because of the time he has to get up for work tomorrow, and Mum was yawning over the computer when I said goodnight. No one knows about this except me, so no one's going to know if I wimp out. Not that it would be wimping out. It is the only sensible thing to do.

But I'm not going to do it. Because if I don't follow this up, I'm not going to sleep tonight, or any other night. I've got to know what this is all about. And if I walk straight into trouble because of it, well, I'll just have to hope that I'm fast enough on my feet to find a way out . . .

It was astonishing how much difference an hour or so made. The harbour areas was in darkness now, the beach barbecue over, and the only signs of life Jay saw as he walked quickly and quietly through the town were two cats and a single slow-moving car.

Despite the turmoil in his mind, he was thinking clearly enough to have brought a fresh and smaller torch, changed flip-flops for trainers and slung a fleece over his shoulder. The last traces of light in the western sky were long gone, so the coast path was pitch dark and the sea almost invisible. But behind him a grey-silver glow was strengthening above the horizon as the moon started to rise. It was nearly full, he calculated; by the time he reached the cove there would be enough light for him to see where he was going without having to give his presence away with the torch.

The walk seemed to take twice as long as it had done earlier with Robyn. The wind had dropped completely now, and the air's stillness felt unnatural. The sea was so quiet that he had to stop and listen hard to hear it at all.

The moon was up when he arrived and the sea was visible again, paler grey with cold silver lines showing where the light caught the lift and fall of the swell. In the cove's narrow inlet it looked like a knife blade. Jay stopped at the top of the beach path and scanned what he could see of the beach. *Tide turned and starting to come in. No sign of anyone down there. No sign of anything at all. But I'm going to make sure, before I go on to the campsite.*

He managed to get down the beach path without either using the torch or losing his footing, and walked silently across the sand towards the tide's edge. The sea was audible now; small waves hissed as they ran in and turned to ripples, and he could hear the heavier slap of water against rocks further out. There were scuffed footprints on the sand, but not enough to suggest that anyone other than he and Robyn had been here. The whole scene was deserted, bleak. It made Jay feel bleak too, and he was about to give up this pointless exercise and return to the path when a sudden glint of silver out to sea caught his eye. A larger ripple, not a wave . . . Some inexplicable instinct moved in Jay and he darted to the shelter of the overhanging cliff, where the moonlight didn't reach.

There it is again . . . Another disturbance. *Definitely* not a wave, and closer in this time. Wishing he had infrared vision, he stared hard into the ambiguous patterns of light and shadow. Then his breath seemed to catch against a blockage in his throat as a shape rose out of the water and waded towards the shore.

It was no more than a vaguely distinguishable silhouette against the moonlit sea. Hair flattened by the water, lying over the shoulders like strands of seaweed . . . *Who?* Jay thought. *Male? Female? Kiran? Or someone else . . . ?* Then something about the way the figure moved struck a familiar chord in his mind. *Whoever it is, I've seen them before. Here. Tonight.*

The figure stopped at the tide's edge and scanned the beach as though looking for something or someone. Jay didn't think. Impulse and a need to know took over, and he emerged from his hiding place and sprinted across the sand. The figure's head turned with a quick, animal movement; moonlight flickered across its face, momentarily highlighting the features—

It is female! I'm sure of it!

Then the swimmer saw him, swung round, and ran straight back into the sea.

'Wait!' Jay yelled. Of course, she took no notice. Thigh-deep, she launched forward, dived under an incoming wave and emerged on the far side, swimming powerfully and fast. Jay swore, kicked off his shoes and flung them behind him, threw torch and fleece in their wake, and went after her.

The water was a cold shock – he was used to wearing a wetsuit – but he ignored it and struck out. There were no rip currents as far as he could judge, but there was a surprisingly big swell, and the tide pushed against him, trying to carry him back to the beach. *Don't waste energy. Even strokes. Cut down the water's resistance as much as possible . . .* Jay was a strong swimmer, but as his head broke surface to take a breath he was dismayed to see that his quarry was faster, increasing the distance between them. He'd never catch up – and even if he did, what then? A physical fight, out here in the middle of the sea? *No chance, unless we both want to drown.*

He made one more effort, putting on the best turn of speed he could achieve. But after a few more strokes he knew it was useless, and he stopped swimming and trod water. He couldn't even see her now. There was only the rise and fall of the swell to an empty horizon. She was gone.

Jay floated where he was for a minute or two, partly to get his breath back and partly because of a vague and unrealistic hope that the girl might reappear. She didn't, and at last he turned in the water and started back towards the shore.

He had swum about five metres when something locked on his ankles from below and pulled downwards, hard.

Taken completely by surprise Jay went under, swallowing seawater and choking. The shock was so great that it obliterated any other reaction, and he panicked. His arms flailed wildly, hands grasping for the surface, and his legs kicked without co-ordination as he struggled to break the grip on his ankles. The grip didn't slacken. If anything it seemed to increase; he felt a second terrific jerk that took him deeper, towards the sea bed. He was blind, he was trying to breathe but there was no air, only water that filled his nose and mouth and burned in his throat. The sea and his own blood roared in his ears and he knew on a horrible, primitive level that he was drowning.

Pain shot through his forearms suddenly, but though he was aware of it, it had no reality, as though it was happening to someone else. For a second or two, his body felt as if it were being pulled in half. Jay twisted, a final struggle against a horrifying death that seemed both impossible and inevitable – and the grip on his straining legs vanished. He felt himself jackknife violently, helplessly. And now something else had locked under his armpits and was dragging him in a different direction . . .

Then a storm of bubbles whirled around him, and

his head broke out of water and into air. There was a dark shape beside him; instinctively he tried to fight it, but the attempt was weak, and from a million miles away he heard a voice gasp, 'Keep still, you idiot! I'm trying to help you!'

The words were followed by a horrible rasping noise that, Jay realized dimly, came from his own throat as he spewed out saltwater and tried to suck in the blessed air. Breathing was such a struggle that he remembered nothing of the next two minutes, until sand grated painfully against his body and he was hauled clear of the sea and dumped, like a sodden sack, on solid ground.

'Come on, come on!' Hands rolled him on to his face and fingers were thrust into his mouth, pulling his tongue forward. Convulsively Jay vomited water again, then a third time, as his ribs were pummelled roughly but efficiently to get the rest out of his stomach and lungs. He didn't know how long it was before the pummelling stopped, but at last it did, and he was helped, more gently, with his eyes still closed, to raise himself on his elbows and make his first attempt at sitting up.

'Here; get this round you.' Something that felt like a towel was draped over Jay's torso. Grateful for its dryness, he hugged it around himself. He couldn't speak yet, but didn't think he would be sick again. His lungs were clear now, and anything he might have had in his stomach was long gone. His brain was trying feebly to put what had happened into some semblance of order, but the memories were vague and confused and nothing seemed to make sense. All that did stand out clearly was that someone had pulled him out of the sea and saved his life.

The voice of his rescuer swam into his consciousness again and for the first time he realized that it sounded familiar. 'I suppose that was your shoes and stuff on the sand? The tide had reached them; I chucked them back out of the way.'

Slowly, groggily, Jay raised his head. His eyes stung and in the deceptive moonlight he could not make out much detail. But the voice *was* familiar, and so was the face in front of him.

Kiran said, 'What the hell were you *doing*, man?'

Kiran had got him to his feet and helped him up the beach to a place where there was shelter among the rocks and the sea wouldn't reach them until high tide. Jay was wearing his own fleece now, with a sweater under it – presumably Kiran's, though he couldn't remember when and how he had put them on. With the towel wrapped round his legs, warmth and circulation were coming back, and apart from the grogginess he didn't seem to be suffering any other after-effects. He had been very, very lucky. And he didn't want to think about what would have happened if Kiran hadn't shown up when he did.

'OK now?' Kiran asked.

He sounds like his old self, and it's freaking me out. Jay tried his voice and found that it worked, sort of. 'Yeah . . . OK now . . .' A shiver went through him and left his muscles throbbing. 'Thanks. Really. I mean . . .'

'Forget it.' Kiran's hands gripped his shoulders and shook gently in a tacit brotherly gesture. 'You're out of there, and that's all that matters. Good practice for me, anyway.' He laughed, though it was unconvincing.

'How come you—' Jay coughed, swore, tried again. 'How come you were down here?'

'Never mind; it's not important.' Kiran said it so quickly that Jay knew he was lying. It *was* important; or at least very significant. Kiran had come to the beach for a reason, and it didn't have – couldn't possibly have – anything to do with his own purpose here.

Jay heaved himself more upright. He was feeling

better every minute, and his head was clearing, too. Then as Kiran started to say, 'We'd better find a way to get you home,' all the confusions and questions abruptly gathered together and his mind clicked into full focus.

'No way.' With surprising strength under the circumstances, he shook off Kiran's hands and shifted out of his reach, at the same time turning to face him directly. 'I'm not going anywhere – except back with you, to your tent.'

Even in the semi-darkness he detected a flicker of unease in Kiran's eyes. 'Sorry,' Kiran said, cautiously, 'I don't know what—'

'Don't give me that crap! You know damned well what I mean. The campsite. Where you've been staying while everyone else thought you were in Brittany. And if whoever was in the tent with you earlier's still there, that's tough, because that's where we're both going.' He coughed as the exertion of the words caught up with him, and Kiran took advantage of the pause.

'I don't know what you're on about, man, but you're obviously pretty woozy—'

'I am *not*! Look, I want some answers! And so we don't waste each other's time, I'll tell you right now that Robyn and I were here earlier, and we *saw* your tent, and we *heard* you.' He paused to allow that to sink in, then delivered the trump card. 'We heard the girl you had in there with you, too.'

Kiran stared at him. 'What?'

Jay couldn't quite interpret the tone of his voice. He sounded genuinely surprised – but was he that good an actor? Then Kiran said, 'There was no one else with me. There never has been, since I got here.'

'Oh, right! Doing impressions, then, were you?'

Anger flared in Kiran's face. 'I said, *there was no one else*!' He took a grip on himself. 'Listen to me, Jay. I've been camping here, while you all thought I was in France; OK, I admit that. But there's no one else involved. I came because . . . because I needed some space. Some time alone.'

'Why?' said Jay.

Kiran sucked a long breath in then let it out slowly. 'You wouldn't understand.'

'And Robyn?'

'She – oh, for God's sake, I don't *know*! Maybe. Maybe not.' Kiran's shoulders sagged and his head dropped. 'But if you think I've been two-timing her, you're *wrong*!'

'I'll tell you what I think,' Jay said, ferociously. 'I think you're a bloody liar!'

Kiran's head came up sharply, but Jay was really

wound up now and continued before he could say anything. 'I know who she is, Kiran. You see, I didn't just hear her voice in your tent, I saw her, too. Right here on this beach, tonight!'

'No!' Kiran's voice rose, almost shrill. 'She wasn't! She can't have been!'

Perhaps it was delayed shock after his narrow escape, but at that moment something in Jay snapped, and his temper went with it. 'Oh, she was!' he snarled. 'I ought to know! Because when she saw me she went into the sea to get away from me, and when I went in after her she tried to bloody *drown* me!'

'No!' Kiran shouted. 'That's not true! You got cramp, that's what happened! No one tried to drown you! There was no one else here!'

'Since when has cramp felt like someone grabbing your ankles and pulling you under?' Jay yelled.

The cliffs had been flinging their voices back in a clash of echoes, and the echoes faded into a sudden, peculiar quiet, broken only by the steadier noise of the sea. Kiran's moon-shadow looked stretched and thin, almost sickly, Jay thought in a strange and short-lived flash of imagination. Then Kiran looked away.

'The tide's coming up on us.' His voice was

expressionless. 'We'd better go back to the tent.'

He wasn't ready to admit it, not quite yet, but Jay knew that he had given in. A little more patience, that was all. And then Kiran would tell him something at least approaching the truth.

'OK,' he said quietly. 'Let's move, then.'

Nine

Kiran hasn't said a word since we left the beach. He just keeps walking, staying a few paces in front of me and not looking back any more often than he has to. I suppose he wants to check I'm still here. But he's not really concentrating on me. He's thinking, hard.

My legs feel weak. I know I'm tired – probably exhausted, which is hardly surprising after what happened – but I'm running on an adrenalin high as well, and that's keeping me going. I don't think I could sleep, even if I wanted to. Everything feels unreal, though. I could really use something hot to drink; it might bring me down to earth.

The campsite's ahead now. Amazing how bright the moon is; I can see the tents clearly. No lights, no sign of movement. Looks as if we're the only ones awake . . .

Kiran lit a canister lamp and, as the tent interior lifted into brightness, Jay sat on the single, rumpled sleeping-bag and gazed around. The tent was a tip, as anyone who knew Kiran might expect, but even among the mess there were no obvious signs that any second person had been here.

'I've got coffee somewhere.' Kiran rummaged in a plastic box, shoving aside a personal stereo, a sodden towel and a pair of sandy wetsuit boots. His voice sounded edgy.

'Thanks.' Jay was still gazing, and abruptly Kiran swung round to confront him.

'I know what you're looking for, and you won't find it. I told you: there hasn't been anyone else here.'

'I wasn't—' Jay began.

'You were. It's written all over your face.' He had found the jar of coffee and savagely wrenched the top off it. 'The truth's weirder, Jay. A *hell* of a lot weirder.'

'Then tell me,' said Jay.

He waited while Kiran filled a saucepan from his water container and set it on the portable gas stove to boil. 'All right,' Kiran said at last, between clenched teeth. 'You said you saw that girl at the cove tonight. Well, maybe you did.'

'Hold on,' Jay cut in. 'What do you mean, "that" girl? Who is she?'

'You know very well who she is.'

'No,' he said, 'I don't.'

'Shit, man, stop this, will you? Stop pussyfooting!'

Kiran's face contorted into anger, but with a strong undertone of fear. 'You *know* what I'm telling you! It was her – the girl we saw drown!'

So he does believe it. For all Robyn and I thought, for all that it's the last thing we'd ever have expected of Kiran, he does believe it.

'Kiran,' Jay said, uneasily, 'there are no such things as ghosts.'

'That's what I thought till a few weeks ago. But I don't think it any more.'

The saucepan started to bubble. Kiran ignored it – didn't even seem to notice it – so Jay turned off the gas and made coffee. There was no milk, but he spooned a lot of sugar into both mugs, then set one down in front of Kiran. Kiran stared at it without focusing. Then he continued.

'She's haunting me, Jay. It started soon after – well, you know when it started; you were there. But it's been getting worse and worse. Everywhere I go, I keep seeing her. Broad daylight, after dark; it doesn't matter, she keeps showing up, like – like she's following me around. I thought at first that she was alive; she'd survived somehow, and . . .' He shook his head helplessly as the logic of that defeated him. 'I mean, she couldn't have done, could she? It isn't possible.'

'No,' said Jay. 'It isn't.'

'Right . . . So then I thought: maybe it's me, maybe I'm imagining it, you know? Or mistaking someone else for her, or . . .' He flung out an arm, nearly knocking Jay's coffee out of his hand. 'All the sensible stuff, I went through *all* of it! But the sensible stuff doesn't *work*.' Kiran drew a deep breath, then forced himself to speak more calmly. 'What's sensible about seeing her, following her round a corner and finding she's vanished into thin air?' He saw Jay's bemused face and smiled humourlessly. 'Yeah, it's happened several times. Living people can't do that, though, can they?'

Jay didn't speak but sipped his coffee. It created a clogging, uncomfortable sensation in his throat.

'That's the really insane thing,' Kiran went on, his voice much quieter now. 'I always follow her. Every time I see her. I don't want to do it, but I can't stop myself; it's like a compulsion. I get this feeling – don't know why, but I do – that she's trying to make me follow her.'

'Yet she disappears every time you try? That doesn't make sense.'

'I *know* it doesn't! But I think it. I can't *stop* thinking it! Look, if you're going to—'

'OK, OK,' Jay interrupted. 'Sorry. Go on.'

Kiran subsided again. 'A couple of weeks ago – just before the Brittany trip – I was heading home from the beach, and suddenly she was right there in front of me on the road. It was getting dark, and I – I kind of freaked. I yelled at her, "What do you want?"'

'And . . . ?'

'She smiled. Don't look at me like that, man, she *did* smile! Then she turned round and walked off towards the coast path.'

'And you went after her?'

Kiran nodded. 'I thought I'd try a different approach. I didn't run after her; I walked. Kept pace. And this time she didn't vanish.' He blew out breath in an effort to loosen his tension. 'I could just about see her on the path ahead of me. I followed her to the cove here. I saw her go down the cliff path; she dropped out of sight, and when I got to the edge and looked, she . . . just wasn't there.'

Jay began to understand. 'So that's why you decided to camp up here?'

'Yeah, that's why. I thought maybe she'd led me here for a reason. I thought I might find some answers.'

But for the subtle hissing of the gas lamp there was silence for a few moments. Jay was aware of an pressing sense of claustrophobia building up in his mind. The cramped confines of the tent, the darkness outside . . . he felt vulnerable suddenly, and wasn't sure why.

Pushing the feeling away as best he could, he said, 'All right. I can see where you're coming from.' His mouth was dry now; he swallowed more coffee but it didn't help. 'Since you came here, has anything else happened?'

'You mean, have I seen her again?' Kiran hunched his shoulders and stared moodily at his own clasped and restless hands. 'I don't know. I *think* I have. But she's always too far away to be sure. Till tonight . . .'

Jay's uneasy feelings deepened. 'What about tonight?'

'About an hour ago, I suppose it must have been . . . I was lying here thinking, and . . . I heard a voice. It was just on the other side of that tent wall – ' he pointed, ' – and it called me by name.'

Jay tried not to notice that Kiran was shivering now. 'A girl's voice?' he asked.

'Yeah. I'd never heard it before. But I *know* it was her.'

'So what did you do?'

Kiran gave a sharp, bitter bark of a laugh. 'What

do you think I did? I was out of here in three seconds flat, looking for her. There was no one there, of course. But I . . . it was as if I could still hear that voice, inside my head, and I had this overwhelming feeling that I had to go to the beach.'

'So you did.'

'Yeah.' Kiran's knuckles turned white as he clenched his locked fingers hard. He met Jay's gaze, his eyes intense and haunted. 'Just as well for you, wasn't it?'

I'm trying to hold his gaze, but I can't; I've got to look away. I don't even know what to think, let alone what to say now. I feel like I'm on a precipice, and the smallest wrong move could send me – or maybe both of us – spinning over the edge. So many pieces, so many things that don't add up or make any rational sense . . . Where do I start trying to understand? But something made Kiran go down to the cove when he did, and if that hadn't happened, I'd probably be dead by now.

Kiran's voice broke in on his thoughts. 'She called me here, Jay. I'm convinced she did. I think she knew you were going to get into trouble, and she wanted me to find you before it was too late.'

Or find me washed up drowned, and laugh about it from somewhere well out of sight . . .

Abruptly, a few of the scattered pieces slotted into

place in Jay's mind, and with it came an ugly and frightening conclusion. Whatever Kiran said, whatever he might have experienced, Jay did not believe in ghosts. But he did believe in evil. Real, tangible, *human* evil.

'What does she *want*?' Kiran sounded like a small child pleading for help. 'I've got to find out, Jay, or I'm going to end up losing my mind!'

And I can't help you, because I haven't got any answers. All I'm sure of is that someone was on the beach tonight, and that same someone tried to drown me. Kiran saved my life – but he wouldn't have gone to the cove unless he'd been led there. It doesn't make any sense. Who is this girl? Why has she targeted us?

And what the hell sort of person are we tangling with?

Jay said, 'We're going back.'

'What?'

'You heard.' Jay was surprised by the vehemence of his own voice. This was a new side to him – in all the years of their friendship he had never before had the nerve to take the upper hand with Kiran, even if Kiran would have allowed it. But a new urgency was driving him. And for the first time in his life he was not about to be argued with.

Because I'm not going to leave him here to be preyed on. We're not talking imagination now. We're not talking merrows. We're talking about a total stranger who could be a homicidal maniac.

'It won't take long to pack up your gear,' he continued, 'and if you carried it here by yourself, it's going to be no problem for two of us.'

'Wait a minute—'

'*No!*' Jay snapped. 'I'm not giving you a choice, man. You come back to town with me, now, or I'm going to tell everyone where you are. Starting with Robyn and your parents. And I'll tell them why you're here, too. That's not exactly going to make you flavour of the month, is it?'

Kiran stared at him as if he could barely believe what he was hearing, and Jay realized that in a perverse way he was almost enjoying this. For a moment, the thought flicked through his head: *I wish Robyn was here to see it*, but he squashed it immediately.

Kiran said, 'That's blackmail.'

'I don't care. I mean it, Kiran. We both leave now, or I rat on you. Your choice.'

It was a gamble, but I was pretty sure he'd give in. One thing Kiran can't bear is looking like a prat in the eyes of his mates; even me. If I did what I threatened, his cred would go straight through the floor and he knew it. Yes, it was blackmail, and I didn't particularly like myself for doing it. But I had to. And it worked.

They started packing in a hostile silence broken only by an occasional clatter or thump as Kiran angrily hurled items into his bag. If the noise disturbed any other campers, no one came to investigate or complain, and before long the whole kit was ready enough to be carried between them without too much trouble.

As Jay zipped the bag containing the tent poles, Kiran walked a few paces away and stood staring moodily towards the sea. The moon was still up, but to the east another, yellower light was starting to show on the horizon.

'Come on,' Jay said, more sharply than he had intended. 'Dawn's not far off, and we both want to get home before it gets too light.'

Kiran did not answer for a few seconds. Then: 'You've forgotten something.'

'What?' Jay straightened up. Kiran had turned to face him. He seemed less angry than he had been a few minutes ago, but there was still a lingering edge of antagonism.

'The Brittany lot don't get back till tomorrow night. So where am I supposed to go until then? Or do you expect me to walk in my front door and say, "Hi, Mum and Dad, I'm in two places at once"?'

'Shit . . .' Jay's face fell. He hadn't thought about that. But Kiran was right. Finding some excuse for friends was one thing; his parents, though, were the sort who asked questions and demanded satisfactory answers.

A part of Jay suggested darkly that if Kiran landed in hot water he only had himself to blame. But he didn't want to think like that – besides, if this problem wasn't sorted, Kiran would use it as an excuse to change his mind about coming back at all. And that, above all, must not be allowed to happen.

He thought rapidly, and a solution came.

'Rick and Charlie Venton both booked on the Brittany trip, didn't they?'

Rick Venton was the senior lifeguard at the beach, and Charlie, his younger brother, was in Jay's year at school. Kiran frowned. 'Yeah, they did. Why?'

'Rick's got one of the beach huts at Porthmazy, and I know where the key is. There's no chance of either of them showing up there for the next couple of days.' Jay shrugged. 'So it's all yours, if you want it.'

Slowly, Kiran's expression relaxed. 'OK. If you can get the key, I'll use it.'

It couldn't have been easier, because Rick's the sort of guy who's always losing things. He's lost the key to the beach hut three times, so – according to Charlie – he's now hung it on a piece of string tied inside the gutter over the door. Thanks, Charlie. I owe you one.

It was another silent walk on the way back, but this time I was glad of it. The adrenalin was running out and everything had started to catch up with me, so that I moved on a kind of autopilot, putting one foot in front of the other but not really aware of it. By the time we reached town it was past five and nearly full daylight. Nothing around except a few cats, though we heard what was probably a newsagent's delivery van in the distance. All the same, we took the back lanes to be on the safe side. I noticed the way Kiran kept glancing nervously around; particularly when we passed the entrance to any of the narrow alleys. Didn't take a genius to work out what was going on in his head. But whatever it was he feared he might see, it didn't show up . . .

They skirted the car park behind the smaller and more private Porthmazy beach, then walked past the closed and silent café, and turned on to the walkway from where a row of beach huts overlooked the sand.

'This is the one.' Jay dumped his share of the camping gear on the ground and reached up to the gutter. The key was there; they let themselves in and Kiran stared around with the air of someone who had just found himself deposited on an alien planet.

'It's a bit bare,' said Jay. 'Most of the stuff Rick normally keeps here has probably gone to Brittany.'

'That's OK.' Kiran's voice was dull. 'I've got my sleeping-bag. That's all I care about right now.'

'I'd better go, then. Get back before Mum and Dad wake up.' Jay hesitated. 'Look, man . . . try not to worry about anything, OK? I'll meet you here in the morning.'

'Sure; whatever. Go on, get going, will you? I need some kip, even if you don't.'

At the door, Jay looked back. Kiran had dragged his sleeping-bag from the haphazard bundle he had been carrying and was draping it on the floor.

'Kiran.'

Kiran looked round. 'What?'

'She isn't going to follow you back here. Keep telling yourself that, right?'

He didn't really know why he had said it. It was a momentary impulse, and at once he wondered if he had been stupid to bring up the subject unnecessarily. But Kiran's expression told him that it hardly mattered. At this moment, there was nothing else on either of their minds.

Kiran said, 'See you later, Jay.' It was a clear dismissal, and a sign that he had no intention of saying another word.

Jay closed the door behind him and for a few moments stood staring down at the empty beach. The tide was high now and slack, licking sluggishly at a fringe of cast-up bladderwrack, and the rising sun dazzled his eyes and made him blink. It was going to be yet another blazing, windless day. The kind of day when the heat haze reflected off every surface and made you see mirages . . .

Rock outcrops formed enclosing arms to either side of the beach, and he imagined, briefly, that he saw someone standing on the left-hand outcrop; standing very still and watching him. There was no one there, of course. It was only the light playing tricks on his tired mind.

Jay turned away from the beach and began the long trudge home.

Ten

So of course, after all the hassle of getting back indoors through the bathroom window and falling into bed, now I can't sleep. I suppose I should have expected it – I've gone past the point of no return where tiredness is concerned, and on top of that my mind's racing with thoughts, questions, worries and everything else.

The one thing that I can't get my head around is how Kiran – solid, unimaginative Kiran – could have got into this state. Ask him, just a few weeks ago, if he believed in ghosts and he'd have laughed in your face. Yet this girl, whoever she is, has twisted his brain right around and got him totally convinced that he's being haunted by a dead spirit.

Kiran's merrow. Who the hell is she? Why's she doing this to him? One possibility I came up with (though no way was I going to say this to Kiran) is that she could be some past girlfriend; someone he dumped, who's got a grudge about it and is out to give him a hard time. But that doesn't add up, does it? I know the girls Kiran had scenes with before Robyn; however much he might have

126

*pissed them off, none of them would play tricks like this.
Aside of anything else, they couldn't be bothered.*

*And that's the other thing that keeps bugging me. I
blackmailed Kiran into packing up camp because I wasn't
going to leave him on his own if that girl might still be
hanging around. 'Homicidal maniac' was the term in
my head. As soon as I'd thought it, I told myself I was
being over the top. But was I? Tormenting a guy for some
kind of kick is warped enough; but last night someone
tried to kill me – and she's the only logical suspect.*

*Now I'm starting to sound like a bad police drama
script. But there's nothing fictional about this, and
nothing to laugh about either. If I'm right about this girl,
then she's dangerous, and she ought to be in a secure
hospital, not running loose.*

*I need to talk to Robyn. Whether Kiran likes it or not,
she's got a right to know what's going on. It's nearly seven;
crazily early, I know, but someone at her place will
probably be up by now. I don't want to phone. This needs
to be said face-to-face. And if she chews me out for waking
her, tough. I can't wait any longer.*

A cold shower was a shock but it washed away some
of the thick feeling in Jay's head. He went downstairs
wet-haired and heavy-eyed; his father was in the
kitchen making tea, but Jay evaded his astonished

questions and simply said that he had something to do before work and would get breakfast at one of the cafés.

He had to stop himself from breaking into a run as he headed towards Robyn's house. There was no real need to hurry; from the way he had looked last night it was a safe bet that Kiran would sleep at least half the morning.

He reached the house and rang the doorbell. Robyn's mother was as surprised as his own father had been, but she didn't ask questions, only shouted up the stairs to Robyn that she had a visitor. A few moments passed while Jay fidgeted in the hall, then Robyn, bare-legged and wearing a long and crumpled T-shirt that she had obviously slept in, appeared at the top of the stairs.

'Jay. . .' Then, tautly, 'Is it Kiran?'

'Yes. Last night, I—'

'Wait there.' She flew back to her room, reappeared seconds later with jeans thrown on, and came down the stairs three at a time. 'What's happened?'

Jay looked at her tense face and wide eyes. After the things she had said last night he had half expected her to declare that she had no more interest in anything Kiran thought or did or said.

But no. She was as anxious as ever about him, if not more so. The old habit hadn't broken and the ties were still there, and Jay hated himself for feeling bitter and rejected.

He started to tell her what had happened, but had spoken hardly more than a few sentences before she interrupted.

'Where is he now?'

'At Rick Venton's beach hut on Porthmazy. You know Rick's brother Charlie; he—'

'Never mind all that!' Robyn swept his efforts aside with an impatient wave of one hand. 'I'm going over there!'

'Robyn, hold on! There's a lot more—'

'It can wait! Hell, where are my *sandals*?' She rummaged among a pile of shoes under the coat rack, found her sandals, kicked them on. 'Are you coming, or are you just going to stand around like a stuffed mackerel?'

Stinging, Jay followed her out of the door and along the street. She didn't wait for him, didn't once glance back at him but headed at a fast, ground-eating stride towards the harbour. Tired as he was, it took all Jay's energy to keep pace with her, and it was only when she slowed down on the hill approaching the car park behind the beach that he was at last able to catch up and take hold of her arm.

'Robyn, listen to me! Before you see Kiran, there are some things you've got to know!'

Perhaps the exertion had knocked back some of Robyn's hot-headedness, because this time she did stop and take his words in. 'What things?'

Where to start? Jay drew breath and decided that bluntness was best; if he tried to approach this gently she would only get impatient again. 'Last night at the cove,' he told her, 'someone tried to drown me. If it hadn't been for Kiran, they'd have succeeded.'

'*What?*' She was certainly listening now. 'Who, Jay? How? I mean—'

He gave her a brief, stark account, beginning with his first glimpse of the girl in the sea and ending at the moment when Kiran had dragged him from the water. Robyn's expression seemed to shrink and close up as he spoke, and when he finished she stood very still for a few seconds, her brows knitted in a tight, painful frown.

At last she said, 'Jay are you sure about this?'

'*Sure?*' Jay's voice went up the scale in outrage. 'Oh no, of course I'm not! Obviously, I imagined it, didn't I? Or maybe I tried to drown myself!'

'That's not what I mean and you know it isn't!' Robyn flared back. 'But couldn't it have been cramp? Or maybe even a seal? You know the way seals sometimes come around when people are surfing; they like to play, but they can play too rough sometimes.'

Well, I'll give Kiran his credit; at least he didn't come up with that excuse . . . 'Robyn,' Jay said, 'someone got hold of my ankles and deliberately pulled me down. Cramp doesn't do that. And seals haven't got hands.'

Her shoulders sagged and she turned away, staring across the all but empty car park. 'OK, I know. I was just . . . looking for another way to explain it.'

'Why look? The answer's staring you in the face. It was her.'

'But that's just it, isn't it? *Her.* Her who?' She ran her tongue over her lower lip. 'You see, I've been doing some thinking, and . . . Jay, I don't think this girl exists at all.'

'Wait a minute; she—'

'No; listen to me. Please.'

Robyn rarely said 'please' to him, and it silenced Jay. She pushed her hands as deep into her jeans pockets as they would go and continued.

'Kiran thinks he's being haunted by a ghost, and you think he's being targeted by a lunatic. I think the truth's something else. There's no lunatic. And the ghost is only in Kiran's head.' She looked at him and tried to smile. 'The mind's a very powerful thing, and very hard to control. Look at me with those automatic drawings. I was probably picking up some kind of signal from Kiran, and that was why I sketched the cove.'

'Like telepathy?'

'Sort of. Though probably not the way people usually think of it; Kiran's been on a guilt trip since that girl drowned. We both know that. He can't come to terms with the fact that he didn't save her, so he's invented this whole crazy scenario about her ghost haunting him, and it's gone so far now that he totally believes it.' She grimaced. 'Remember what you told me about merrows? Well, he's made his very own. He's punishing himself. He thinks the girl's come back to accuse him, and he thinks he deserves it. So he's just given in and let it happen. Or rather, *made* it happen.'

It was plausible, Jay thought. In fact it came closer to a rational explanation than anything else they had thought of so far.

But . . .

'Hold on,' he said. 'What about the other voice we heard in Kiran's tent?'

Robyn's face tightened with a pained reflex – but she had an answer. 'It was Kiran,' she said firmly. 'Jay, it must have been! If he's that far gone, imagining – he was talking to himself, but in his head he was talking to his merrow and making her answer.'

'So who did we see at the cove last night?'

She didn't waver. 'Kiran.'

'And when I went back on my own?' Jay demanded. 'Was that Kiran, too?'

Robyn hesitated. Then: 'Jay . . . I don't think you saw anyone that second time.'

'*What*? Hey, hang on! *I'm* not on a guilt trip; I don't go around imagining people who aren't there! She was *real*.'

'Was she?' Robyn countered. 'You *thought* you saw her, and you *thought* you followed her into the sea. But it's the mind again, isn't it? We'd already had one bad experience when we went to the cove together. Then you went back, and instead of daylight there was moonlight, which makes everything look strange. And you must have been tired by then, and you were already caught up in Kiran's weirdness. That's just the sort of situation where your imagination *can* catch you out. Isn't it possible that you imagined her, Jay? *Isn't* it?'

'But there was *something* there.'

'Like I said, it could have been a seal. Or even a dolphin. But I'm sure, Jay, I'm absolutely sure that it was *not* her. Because I truly don't believe she exists outside Kiran's head.'

Could Robyn be right? The more I listen to her, the more I want to agree with her theory. I was in a bit of a state last night; not only tired but stressed out and jumpy as well. And yes, I understand what she means about the mind playing tricks. The only thing is—

Robyn broke into his thoughts before he could fully gather them. 'Look, at the moment there's only one thing that matters, right? We've got to get Kiran through this and out the other side in one piece. And it's not a good idea to leave him on his own in the beach hut for any longer than we need to.' She started across the car park towards the beach slope, then looked back. 'Are you coming?'

There was so much more Jay wanted to say and explore while he had the chance. But the abrupt change in Robyn's manner killed his hopes. Kiran was the only one she cared about in any real sense. The knowledge wasn't new, but it came home to him hard all the same.

'Yeah,' he said, suddenly feeling that he could lie down where he was and sleep for a month. 'I'm coming.'

There was no answer when Robyn knocked at the beach-hut door, but that, Jay thought, was hardly surprising.

'He'll still be right out,' he said. 'He's only had a couple of hours' sleep.' *Which is a couple of hours more than I've had. But Robyn hasn't even thought of that.*

'OK; then we'll just have to disturb him.' Robyn tried the handle, but the door would not open. 'He must have locked it from the inside,' she said. 'Oh, hell . . . Kiran! *Kiran!*'

'Don't shout like that; you'll wake everyone within half a mile!'

'So what? This is more important.' She called Kiran's name again, rattling the handle as if that would make any difference. There was no sound from inside the hut, and with an exasperated – or perhaps apprehensive – sigh, Robyn moved to the window and peered in, cupping her hands against the glass.

'I can't see him.' Now she *did* sound worried.

'Look for a heap in one corner,' Jay suggested sourly.

She flashed him an angry look. 'That's not helpful.' A tremor crept into her voice. 'I don't think he's there. I think he's gone! Look, are you sure this is the right hut?'

'Of course I am!' Jay's temper was beginning to fray at the edges now. 'Look at the gutter; you can see the string tied round it where Rick puts the key.' Then, for no logical reason, a thought occurred to him. He reached up, curling his fingers over the gutter's edge . . . and felt the contours of a small metal object.

He withdrew his hand with the key in it and showed it wordlessly to Robyn. She gave him another look, but this one was a raw mixture of bemusement and dread. Then she snatched the key and inserted it in the lock.

Kiran had gone. The jumble of his camping kit was still where Jay had last seen it, and the sleeping-bag looked as if it had been used very recently. But that was all.

Robyn stood in the middle of the room with her hands over her face and swore, softly but savagely, over and over again until Jay took hold of her shoulders and made her stop.

'Where is he?' She was close to tears. 'Where's he *gone*?'

Knowing Kiran, Jay's guess was that he'd simply changed his mind about staying at the hut. But he was wise enough to know how Robyn would react to any implied slur, so said nothing. She had pulled away from him now and was searching feverishly through Kiran's belongings. Unable to imagine what she thought she might find there, Jay turned slowly on one heel, his gaze travelling over the walls and window of the hut.

Then he saw a piece of paper wedged in the window catch.

He crossed to the window and pulled the paper free. The outside was blank, but when he unfolded it he immediately recognized Kiran's sprawling handwriting.

Jay, Kiran had written, **I can't hole up here, because I know you'll bring Robyn and I don't want to face her. Couldn't say this to you before, but I'm shit-scared. Baggage goes with you unless you can find a way of getting rid of it once and for all, and I've just found out that I'm not up to doing it until I've had more time to work this through. Sorry to mess you around. And sorry about what happened to you at the cove. Believe me when I say I didn't mean that to happen. K.**

'Let me see it!' Robyn had come up behind Jay,

startling him; she all but snatched the paper from him and read it fast. Then she palmed her mobile and called Kiran's number.

'It's switched off . . .'

'It would be, wouldn't it? You saw what he said – he doesn't want to talk.'

'And he says he's shit-scared.' Robyn started to pace, her steps noisy on the wooden floor. 'Where is he, where *is* he?' She stopped. 'What about the campsite?'

'No way,' said Jay with certainty. 'He knows it's the first place we'd think of. Anyway, all his gear's here. And before you say it, I don't think he's at the cove, either.' *Not after last night.*

Robyn subsided but didn't speak again. Instead she pressed herself to the doorpost and began to knock her forehead against it, not hard but with savage emphasis.

'Hey, stop that!' Jay put his hands on her shoulders, pulled her away and turned her forcibly to face him. Their gazes met; Jay's saw the glitter of tears welling in Robyn's eyes, and a flashback to the cove beach, standing with her in his arms, the way she had let him hold her, the knowledge that at that moment she had *needed* him, overturned his self-control. He reached out for her, his voice husky with the feelings that were running through him.

'Robyn, you know I—'

'Don't!' She flinched back, as though from a poisonous snake. The tears stopped welling and the look in her eyes changed from unhappy confusion to anger and accusation.

'I'm sorry!' Jay said in consternation, cursing himself for every kind of idiot on the planet. 'I only—'

'Don't tell me. I don't want to know.' She turned away, her posture rigid and hostile. 'Not now, not at any time. Message understood?'

And I suppose it was at that moment that I finally had to stop kidding myself and accept how much Kiran really means to her.

'Message understood,' he said, bleakly. 'I'm sorry.'

'No need. Just forget it, and shut up. *Please.*' She shook herself as though casting off some invisible, restricting cloak. 'I'm going to start looking for Kiran.'

Even then, Jay couldn't stop himself from trying one last time. 'You ought to get some breakfast first,' he said. 'What about the Blue Reef?'

'I haven't got any money on me.'

'I'll pay—'

She stopped him with a look that killed the last ghosts of his hopes. 'No, Jay. You heard what I said, and I meant it. No.'

There was silence for a few moments. Then, trying to keep his voice even, Jay said, 'Where are you going to start looking?'

She shrugged. 'Surf club, maybe. Craster beach, anyway.' Her eyes burned again. 'And before you say it, I'd rather you didn't come with me, OK?'

'OK.' Jay let out a resigned sigh. 'Shall I call you later?'

'Only if there's any news,' said Robyn, and went.

Eleven

So that was how we left it. What other choice did I have? When Robyn had gone, I stood in the middle of the hut and used every obscenity I could think of on Kiran. It didn't make me feel much better, but at least it got the worst of the anger out of my system.

Even if Robyn didn't want me going with her, I wondered if maybe I ought to search for Kiran myself. But then I thought: why should I give a toss where he is or what he's doing? Whatever Robyn might fear, he's more than capable of looking after himself, and he will. Kiran always comes out on top. To hell with him. I'm not going to run around in his shadow any more.

There wasn't much point in going back home, so I headed to Craster, getting myself a takeaway coffee and doughnut on the way. OK, I admit I thought Robyn might be there – she wasn't – and I did take a quick look around the surf clubhouse (called myself an idiot for doing it), but there was no sign of Kiran either. Even after that I was half an hour early for work. Steve looked at me as if he was hallucinating and made the obvious wisecracks; I just smiled – sort of – and started doing some unpacking in the stockroom.

I held out till eleven-thirty before, finally, I couldn't stop myself from calling Robyn. No reply. Probably she saw my name come up and decided not to answer. Steve told me to take lunch early. He'd stopped the wisecracks by then, and he could obviously see that I wasn't exactly firing on all cylinders, though he didn't ask about it. I thought about surfing but didn't trust myself in the sea after a night of no sleep, so I just sat on the beach for a bit, probably (subconsciously) watching for Robyn. She didn't show, though, and what with the heat and intense light – it's been another of those blistering days – and the background noise of the holiday crowds and the sea . . . well, it all merged together and, the next thing I knew, Steve was prodding me with his foot and telling me to wake up before I cooked myself.

I went home after that. Steve's orders; he said I looked like death warmed over and the shop could survive the afternoon without me. Appreciate that, Steve. I had one more try at calling Robyn, but again she didn't answer her mobile to me. I didn't know if she'd had any luck tracking Kiran down, and I was far too knackered to care. I went home, and just made it to my bed before everything blanked out.

Then when I woke up – around five, I think it was –

the thought was in my head, and I couldn't make it go away . . .

Jay found Kiran's note in his pocket. He must have taken it without consciously realizing, but the fact that it *was* there seemed, to him, to add an unpleasant significance and emphasis to the thing that had risen in his mind and now refused to leave him alone.

His parents were not yet home from work, so he went down to the kitchen and made a pot of strong coffee that he hoped would clear some of the clutter of tiredness, delayed shock and general confusion in his brain. The house felt hot; the afternoon was abnormally still, and even with every door and window flung open there didn't seem to be enough air to breathe. Jay's scalp itched from last night's saltwater that he hadn't yet washed out of his hair. His eyes itched too, and there was a background ringing in his ears that he found distracting.

But not so distracting that it stopped him from dwelling on the note, and the thoughts that had taken shape in his mind while he slept.

Robyn's earlier words – or the gist of them – kept coming back to him. She believed that there was no ghost, and no psychotic girl on the loose, but the 'haunting' was happening entirely in Kiran's mind. It was a plausible theory, and certainly more rational than any of the others. But it left the question: Who had Jay seen coming out of the water when he returned to the cove? It was pushing logic too far to believe that he had imagined it and there was no one there at all. That was one of the things he had been unable to accept about Robyn's argument. So who was it?

The obvious answer was Kiran. At the time, Jay had been convinced that the indistinct figure on the beach was female. But – as Robyn had pointed out – it had all happened by moonlight, and Jay was overwrought. He had half expected to see the girl, hadn't he? A shape coming out of the sea. Wet hair flopping on shoulders. Kiran's hair was shoulder length, too, though he usually wore it tied back in a tail. In the circumstances, wouldn't it have been all too easy to make a mistake?

But if the mystery swimmer *was* Kiran, that led to a horrible conclusion. That it must have been Kiran who had tried to drown him . . .

Jay stood staring at the brewing coffee, wondering if he had finally and completely lost the plot. An inner voice was yelling, *That's insane, you're crazy, you've totally flipped*. But the voice was being eroded by another, stronger impulse as the idea really began to sink in; and suddenly, horribly, his brain started to come at it from a different direction.

Segments of Kiran's note lodged in his memory. Kiran had said 'sorry' and 'I didn't mean that to happen'. What had he meant by 'that'? Though he didn't want it to, a scenario was unfolding in Jay's mind. Kiran had seen him, knew his secret was discovered and didn't want to be challenged. The sea was the only way out of a confrontation; but Jay followed him. Panic set in, a moment's aberration, and without taking time to think about the consequences Kiran had dived, grabbed Jay from below and pulled him under. Probably the idea was to give him a scare, only it went wrong. Kiran came to his senses in time, realized what he had nearly done, and got Jay out of trouble and back to the beach.

Was that possible? Jay didn't want to believe it. Kiran just wouldn't pull that kind of stunt; it wasn't in him to do it. But then the inner voice came back: *Not in his right mind, no. But think about the state he's been in these last few weeks. Since this whole thing started, it's as if he's become a different person altogether. A stranger. It can be a big mistake to assume that you know what a stranger will or won't do.*

And Robyn had gone looking for him . . .

Snatching his mobile from the worktop where he had put it, Jay called Robyn's number again. She had to know about this, right now – never mind the consequences; she could yell at him, call him a liar, refuse ever to speak to him again, it didn't matter. He *had* to warn her.

Robyn's phone rang and rang, but for the third time that day she didn't answer. *OK*, Jay told himself, trying to keep calm, *it's the same thing as this morning; she knows it's me and she doesn't want to talk to me, so she's ignoring it. Let it be that. Please, God, let it be that.*

And if it wasn't . . . ?

He was out of the house in less than three minutes and heading at a run into town. He had almost reached the lifeboat house at the near end of the harbour when it occurred to him that this impulsive rush to find Robyn was pointless. She could be anywhere; town, beaches – she could even (though he didn't want even to consider this) have gone back to the campsite cove in case Kiran was there. Jay slowed down, then stopped by the railing overlooking the lifeboat slipway. Breathing hard, he tried to think. Who might have seen Robyn? Who might have some idea of where she was? The gallery where she worked could be a starting point . . .

He set off again, not running now but at a fast walk, and turned into the maze of streets that formed the heart of the town. Everywhere was busy, even the small lanes, and a lot of his breath went in apologizing to people he collided with. The gallery was not far, but it was uphill all the way and by the time he reached the street he wanted, his skin was covered by a film of sweat. Though evening was not far off, the heat of the day showed no sign of lessening. But the sky was changing; an oppressive, brassy haze had begun to taint the blue, and the sun shining through it had a tarnished look. It bore all the hallmarks of a building thunderstorm, but Jay gave it no more than a momentary thought as the gallery's sign board came in sight ahead of him.

The shop was open but Robyn was not there. A tall woman – not the owner but someone Jay didn't know – said that Robyn hadn't shown up for work today, then added, with more than a trace of sarcasm, that this was actually an art gallery and not a convenient meeting place for half the town's surfers. Jay muttered something that might or might not have been an apology, but as he walked away, her words stuck in his mind. Surfers. The club. It was possible that Robyn had been there, and that someone had talked to her...

At the beach, the lifeguards' day had finished and they were packing up. Jay saw Greg in the distance, carrying the warning flags on their poles back to the clubhouse, and he cut across the sand to meet him.

'Yeah, Robyn was around a bit earlier,' Greg said, in response to his question.

'When?' Jay asked.

Greg gave him a curious look. 'I don't know. Couple of hours ago, maybe?'

'But you haven't seen her since then?'

'No, mate; I've been too busy.' Greg started to walk away, then glanced back. 'She might be in surfing.'

'Oh – yeah. Right. Cheers.'

Jay stared at the sea. There were at least two-dozen wetsuited figures in with their boards, and if Robyn was among them he was not long-sighted enough to pick her out. Where *was* she? He should have asked Greg to call her; she might answer her mobile to him. But what if she didn't? What if she couldn't for some reason? Say she'd found Kiran, confronted him, tried to talk sense into him. If Kiran could do something stupid once, he could do it a second time . . .

Jay swore under his breath and thrust that thought away. There were so many different conundrums going round in his head that he was starting to feel like banging his skull against the nearest wall. Kiran's behaviour, his whereabouts now, the possibility that Robyn could be putting herself at risk . . . and for the last few minutes something else had been scratching away at the back of his mind, too. He couldn't grasp hold of it, but he knew there was something in his theory about Kiran that didn't add up.

The haze over the sky was thickening. There *would* be a thunderstorm before too long, and the pressure build-up was probably partly to blame for his inability to think clearly. *OK. Greg said Robyn might be surfing. So go in and look for her. At least it's a start.*

He took his own board from the clubhouse and, not bothering with a suit, waded into the water and started to paddle out. Beyond the surf he sat up, legs straddling the board as it lifted and dropped on the swell. A few people waved a friendly acknowledgement to him, but he couldn't see Robyn. Disconsolate and feeling increasingly worried, he kept looking until a voice he knew called out to him, and he screwed round on the board to see Jodie paddling towards him.

'Hi, Jay.' Jodie, too, sat up, shaking water from her hair. 'Caught any?'

He shook his head. 'I haven't been trying. You don't know if Robyn's around, do you? Greg said she might be in.'

'Haven't seen her. Shouldn't think anyone's going to stay much longer now, though.' Jodie nodded towards the southwest. 'We're going to get the grandmother of all storms soon, by the look of that sky.'

Jay looked. The coastline stretching away was reduced to a vague blur against a murky backdrop, and the sky had a sulphurous tint now. Shadows had vanished, he realized, and the light level on the beach had dropped noticeably.

'Pity, really,' Jodie was saying. 'The surf's starting to get up a bit for the first time in days; it could have been good tonight. But I don't fancy being in the sea with lightning around. Remember those three guys the year before last, who were surfing during a storm and nearly got electrocuted?'

'Yeah . . .' Jay was only half listening. He had turned to stare shorewards again, and something had caught his eye.

'Any message for Robyn, if I see her?' Jodie asked.

'Uh? Oh – er . . .' What was the point? 'No, not really. Thanks.'

'OK. See you later.' Jodie's board swung away and she paddled towards the beach.

Other surfers had seen the darkening sky and were going inshore too, but Jay stayed where he was, eyes narrowed as he peered at the still-crowded beach. He must have been mistaken. The Brittany party wouldn't be back until after midnight tonight. Everyone thought Kiran was with them, so surely he wouldn't give himself away by showing up here? But Jay was as certain as it was possible to be from this distance that the solitary figure he had just seen walking between two colourful family encampments *was* Kiran.

Then logic kicked in and he thought, *Hang on: it's going to come out tomorrow anyway, and then they'll all know that Kiran didn't go to France. He must realize that. So maybe he's just decided to get the rows over with.*

Or maybe there's another reason why he's here . . .

A wave was rising behind him, and on impulse he swung the board round and lay flat as the green-blue wall of water humped up behind him. He caught the wave and rode it in without standing; in the shallows he jumped off the board and waded ashore.

All the beachgoers had seen the changing sky now and were starting to pack up and leave. Looking for a single individual was nearly impossible with so much activity going on, but Jay wove a way through the flurries towards the far end of the beach. No sign of Kiran. Had he been mistaken? *Like I was at the cove last night?*

Then suddenly he saw the familiar figure again, and there could be no doubt about it. Kiran was standing alone by the far headland, longboard on the sand beside him, watching as the last surfers made their way out of the water. He was wearing his wetsuit but his hair was dry. So he hadn't been in yet.

'Kiran!' Jay broke into a run. Kiran's head turned, and as he drew closer Jay could see the hostile expression on his face.

'What do you want?' Kiran said aggressively, as Jay reached him.

Jay didn't bother with any niceties. 'Where's Robyn?' he demanded.

'How the hell should I know where she is? Or care?' Muscles worked in Kiran's jaw and neck. 'You just had to go and blab everything to her, didn't you? Send her scurrying after me, all whingeymumsy: "I want to help you, Kiran, why won't you talk to me, Kiran, I think you're going mental, Kiran"' – his voice changed viciously to a little-girly whine as he mimicked.

'I only—'

'Bollocks! You didn't "only" anything; you poked your nose in where it wasn't wanted, as usual! Look, *mate*, if I want any help – which I don't – I'll bloody ask for it! Sure, I'm sick – sick of the pair of *you*! So just leave me alone from now on, right?'

The full implication of what he had said hit Jay then. *Send her scurrying after me* – Robyn had found him, tried to talk to him.

His teeth clenched and he repeated, 'Where's Robyn? What have you done?'

'*Done?*' Kiran shouted, turning nearby heads. 'What do you mean, *done*? What are you on about, man?'

Jay's saner self knew that he shouldn't react as he did, but he was so angry, so afraid, that he couldn't make himself stop. 'You know what I'm on about!' he snapped back. 'What did you do to her, Kiran? Same as you did to me last night? Give us both a scare, teach us a lesson, so we'll keep out of the way and let you play with your crazy obsessions all by yourself?'

Kiran stared. Then his face changed, and Jay saw that he had understood. *Oh, shit*, he thought, *what have I said? I've just accused him of nearly killing me, and he knows it . . .*

At last Kiran spoke. He didn't shout; in fact his voice was so low and quiet that Jay could barely hear him. He said, 'You're out of your mind. Seriously, terminally, out of your mind.'

'Kiran, I didn't mean—'

'Oh, you did.' Kiran paused, then jabbed a forefinger against his own brow. 'You think this is all going on in my head, don't you? Kiran's not only gone nuts, he's turned homicidal, too. So you think it was me who dragged you under last night, do you? Fine. Maybe it was. And maybe I've done something to Robyn, too.' He laughed on a strange, high-pitched note. 'Yeah, that'd fit your theory and make you happy, wouldn't it? You could go round saying "told you so" to everyone.'

'Kiran—'

'*Shut up!* I don't want to hear any more!' Bending to the sand, Kiran picked up his longboard. Instinctively Jay flinched back, half expecting the board to come swinging at his head. But Kiran only smiled sourly and tucked it under his arm. 'Don't worry; I'm not having another maniac moment. And if I was, I wouldn't bother with a pathetic little shit like you.'

Hefting the board, he shoved Jay aside and started to walk away. Jay stared wretchedly after him, unable to move or speak. Then Kiran stopped and looked back over his shoulder with a face as thunderous as the sky.

'In case it makes you feel any better, I left Robyn sitting in the café near the car park, with a tragic look on her face and her coffee going cold. She might stay there all night, or she might go home, or she might jump off a cliff. I don't know which, and right now I don't give a toss. I've just got one message for you *and* her – *get off my back*!'

Twelve

She was still at the café. The relief I felt when I saw her sitting there nearly took the breath out of me. My heart was thumping after the encounter with Kiran, and fear for Robyn had been piling on top of that; I just flopped on to the chair next to hers and said something totally cretinous like, 'Thank God you're OK'. She came back at me like a Rottweiler; of course she was OK, why shouldn't she be – which proved she wasn't – and we nearly ended up rowing but just managed to get ourselves back from the brink in time.

I had to tell her what had happened, what I'd said to Kiran; and that meant owning up to my speculations about the business at the cove. To tell the truth, I was thankful to get it out in the open. I realized that I'd badly needed to talk to someone, Robyn most of all. Under the circumstances, though, she was just about the last choice I should have made. But I didn't think of that until it was too late.

Robyn said, 'You pillock. You absolute, total, stupid *pillock*!'

Jay's face was a picture of dismay. He tried to get a word in, but she wasn't interested in explanations or excuses.

'First off you come up with an insane idea like that, and then you go and *tell* him about it?' She flung her hands up in exasperation. 'Where are you *coming* from, Jay? The state Kiran's in, it's the *worst* thing you could possibly have done!'

'Kiran's state was the reason *why* I did it!' Jay protested. 'I was afraid for you! If he's done something stupid once, he might do it again!'

'If, if, if! But he didn't do it! He couldn't have done, he *wouldn't*!'

Not in his right mind, no. Jay's own thought came back to him, but he realized that there was no point in trying to argue with Robyn. She was prejudiced, almost blinded, by her feelings for Kiran. Even if he could prove his accusation she would still refuse to accept it.

She was speaking again, softly and savagely. 'I can't *believe* this. Saying Kiran tried to drown you – he *saved* you, for God's sake!'

'I know he did, but–'

'If anyone's out of their mind at this moment, it's you, not him. All right, all right – ' as Jay opened his mouth again ' – listen to me.' The heels of her hands came down hard on the table. 'I'm not saying there's nothing wrong with Kiran. I know there is. But this crazy idea of yours is all wrong! To do something like that would mean that he – he isn't Kiran any more. And that's not true. It's *not.*'

Though she didn't mean it to show, there was a piteous note in her voice. Jay had learned his lesson now though, and kept quiet.

'Look,' Robyn continued, 'if *my* theory's right, and I know it is, then it's all down to this guilt thing. That's why he yelled at you a few minutes ago, and why . . .'

'He yelled at you, too?' Jay asked, gently.

She hesitated, then nodded, following it with a shrug that implied it hadn't been serious and meant nothing. Jay knew she was lying. Her expression, her manner, gave away the nature of the things Kiran had said to her, even if she would never repeat the words.

She's breaking up inside; hurting so badly. And there's nothing I can do to make it better.

'There's only one way to help him,' Robyn said. 'And it's the opposite of what you did. He's got to be taken through it and out the other side.'

'I don't understand.'

'No, you wouldn't. But *I* do. He's afraid to go near

the Finger again, did you know that? He won't admit it, but he always surfs at the other end of the beach now. If he's ever going to get out of this, he's got to face what happened, face it properly and work it through. If he doesn't, the fear'll just go on growing until it's so much a part of him that he'll never get rid of it.' She paused, staring blindly at nothing. 'I tried to tell him earlier. I tried to explain and make him see that I'm right. But he wouldn't listen.'

'Robyn, I—'

She interrupted, standing up as she did so. 'I'm not going to say any more about it now. I want some time to think.' She checked the bill that was lying on the table, then put it back and dropped some coins on top of it. 'Stay here and have a coffee. You look like you need it, and there's enough there to pay for another one. I'll see you sometime.'

'Robyn—'

'What?' She looked at him. Her face was taut, her eyes over-bright.

'I want to—'

'You can't. See you around, Jay.'

And she went.

It took all my willpower not to run after her right there and then. Only the fact that I knew I'd really blown it stopped me. Even so, I waited only until she was just out of sight before I got up and followed.

When I reached the road that runs behind the beach I saw her ahead of me, moving against the general traffic of people coming off the sand. I still followed but I didn't hurry – I was afraid if I got too close she'd look back and see me, and that would really put the lid on it. At the end of the road, she went down the beach steps. I stopped, gave it a minute and then leaned over the railing to see which way she'd turned.

I mistimed it. Robyn had disappeared.

Jay put his elbows on the rail and his head in his hands, and cursed himself. Then he straightened and started to think things through. OK: Robyn was somewhere on the beach. So, probably, was Kiran. It hardly mattered which of them he looked for first; neither was going to give him a friendly reception anyway. For now at least, his best option was to stay where he was and keep his eyes open.

The beach was almost deserted now. The lifeguards had gone, the shop was locked up and shuttered, and though the surf club door stood open there were no lights on inside. The sky looked filthy. Though he wasn't absolutely sure, Jay had thought he heard a grumble of thunder in the far distance a few minutes ago. The storm was taking its time in coming, but it was certainly on the way. Another hour, maybe less . . . There didn't seem a lot of point in standing here waiting for it to break and soak him. Better to go home.

All the same, he did stay. The last holiday stragglers passed him with their children and dogs and beach gear, grumbling about the weather and giving him idly curious glances which he ignored. Robyn did not reappear, and at last no one at all was left on the sand. Then there was a momentary flicker in the sky down coast, and a few seconds later Jay definitely did hear far-off thunder.

This is stupid. It's so murky I can hardly see the beach anyway, and any minute now it's going to piss down with rain. Go home, Jay. Stop being a prat; go home and forget the whole thing.

He was about to take his own silent advice, turn away and leave, when he saw something moving by the cliffs to his left, at the beach's far end. Jay tensed, peering. The light was so tricky that it would be easy to imagine movement and see shapes where none existed. But he wasn't mistaken. There *was* someone there. A single figure, wearing a wetsuit and carrying a longboard.

Kiran? Impossible to be sure from here. Wishing he had a pair of binoculars, Jay watched as the figure moved clear of the cliffs and walked towards the sea. There was something familiar about it. The striding walk. Long hair, tied back . . .

Long, wet hair, laying like seaweed on the shoulders . . .

Jay's stomach contracted as a flashback of the scene at the cove last night skimmed through his mind. *It looks the same. There was moonlight then and storm light now, but it looks the same.*

Kiran – if it was Kiran – had reached the sea's edge and was wading in. Surf broke over him (it was getting up, as Jodie had said); he breasted the first two waves, the board floating beside him, then he scissored himself on to it and headed out.

A gust of wind blew in Jay's face; the first he had felt for a couple of days and a small warning of the advancing change in the weather. Kiran was a good way out by this time, past the surf and into the swell. Then the board turned and he used his hands to keep it there, waiting.

Jay's mobile rang. It was so unexpected that it made him jump. He took it from his pocket, looked at the screen and couldn't believe what he saw.

'Robyn?' His voice cracked, almost squeaking.

'Jay I want you to listen. Kiran's in the sea—'

So it was him. 'I know,' said Jay. 'I can see him.'

She laughed cynically. 'Yeah, I thought you'd be

hanging around here somewhere. OK; that makes things simpler. I want you to go out there too, and give him a message.'

'Uh? Robyn, what are you—'

'I said, *listen*! I tried to talk to him again just now but he's not hearing me.' Her voice, he realized then, was overloaded with emotion. 'Get to him, and tell him . . . tell him he's got fifteen minutes to find me. And then I'm going to jump.'

'What?' Jay yelled. 'What do you mean, jump? Robyn, what are you talking about?'

'He'll know,' she said, and cut the connection.

Naturally enough, the first thing Jay did was try to call her back. But Robyn had switched her mobile off, and a sick sense of fear started to rise from the pit of Jay's stomach and into his chest. What had she meant? What was she going to *do*?

Kiran would know. Her last words; that he would know . . . Suddenly Jay knew, too; knew exactly what Robyn was planning. And his fear swelled into blind terror.

He ran. Down the beach steps at a breakneck pace and to the surf clubhouse. No one around – but on one of the benches were two piles of clothes, and a mobile. *Robyn's? No time to check, no time for anything* – Jay made to get his own longboard, then instead dragged out one of the lifeguards' rescue boards. *It's bigger, faster, there are grab-handles* – for good measure he also snatched up a torpedo-shaped flotation aid, then he was out of the clubhouse and dragging the board over the sand.

A flurry of rain came in from the sea as he reached the tide's edge. Lightning had glimmered through the windows twice more while he was in the clubhouse, and the interval between the flashes and the thunder was shorter. Jay looked frantically around for Kiran, Robyn, *anyone*, but he could hardly see now; the massive cloud-bank cast a false twilight over everything and only the moving white lines of the surf showed up clearly.

Fifteen minutes ... He had two choices: find Robyn, or find Kiran. Robyn could hide in any one of a dozen places; to search for her would be to waste precious time. But Kiran was in the sea. He was the better bet; the only bet.

And pray to God that he'll listen!

A wave came in and Jay threw the board down on the undertow, running with it and climbing on as it was pulled out into deeper water. Another wave broke over him and he nearly turned broadside to it, just saving himself from being swept off and into the sea. The swell was bigger than it had looked from on shore, and he wasn't used to the size or weight of the rescue board. Well, he'd just have to learn, and fast.

The board seemed to be fighting him rather than working with him, but Jay got it under control and headed out to sea. In the near-darkness it was nearly impossible to distinguish between water and sky, but as he cleared the last of the breakers, a massive flash of lightning lit the entire beach as brightly as noon, and he saw Kiran on his board some twenty metres away.

'Kiran!' Jay paddled with all his strength, closing the gap between them.

'*Go to hell!*' The answering shout came back a second before thunder eclipsed every other sound. Jay powered on, and when the echoes had rolled away he yelled again, 'Kiran! This is urgent!'

Perhaps the desperation in Jay's voice got through to Kiran, for suddenly he turned his board. They closed together – then, in the classic way of Cornish weather, the heavens suddenly and violently opened. Rain battered down as though someone had turned a titanic hose on at full pressure, pounding on their heads and shoulders, hitting the sea with a deafening hiss and churning the surface as if the water was boiling.

Jay heard Kiran's yell above the noise of the elements: 'What the hell are you doing out here? What do you want?'

'It's Robyn!' Jay shouted back. 'She called me – Kiran, she's going to do something stupid, and I can't find her—'

'That's your problem!'

Jay refused to give up. 'You've *got* to help me! Robyn sent a message for you – she says you've got fifteen minutes to find her, or she'll jump!'

'What?' Kiran hadn't heard clearly.

'I said, she'll *jump!*' Jay bawled again, frenziedly. 'It's her stupid, crazy idea of trying to help you! *She's going to jump off the Finger, the same way that girl did!*'

Sheet lightning flickered far out to sea, lasting long enough for Jay to see Kiran's face. It was rigid, angry – and closed. Their eyes met, clashed, then Kiran said, 'She won't do it!'

'You don't know that! What if—'

'I said, *she won't*! I know what she's trying to do, and I'm not falling for it! You go and sort her out if you seriously think she means it – but I'm telling you now, she doesn't, because she's not that dumb!'

Jay stared at him in disbelief. 'Well, I'm going to get her!' he shouted. Then his fury spilled over uncontrollably. 'And if anything goes wrong, if *anything* happens to her, then I'm going to come after you and break your *neck*!'

He turned his board and propelled it away. He neither knew nor cared whether Kiran called out any reply; at this moment the hatred and contempt in him was too strong for anything to get through. The rain was like hammers on his back as he cut through the swell, across the run of the tide and towards the opposite end of the beach. *How much time have I got left? Robyn, don't do this; don't, don't, don't . . .*

He saw the dark line of the Finger ahead of him, looking like a half-submerged sea creature lying in the water. At first, with a flood of relief, he thought there was nothing else there. Then the relief was smashed aside as he realized he was wrong.

Robyn, in shorts and a bikini top, was at the seaward end of the rock. She was on all-fours, hunched against the rain, and in another distant lightning flash Jay saw by her profile that she was looking out across the water, as though searching for something or someone.

He screamed her name, but his cry was lost in the thunder's drum-roll. He was having real difficulty in handling the rescue board now; there was a rip current at this end of the beach, and tonight it was particularly strong. It was pulling the board dangerously close to the mass of smaller, hidden rocks that surrounded the Finger. He *had* to keep clear; if he let himself be carried in too close, the current could all too easily snatch control out of his hands, and if he hit those rocks, he and the board would be smashed to oblivion.

'Robyn! *Robyn!*' He shouted now with all the power his lungs could give.

This time, she heard him. He saw her head turn, her posture change, alert, eager. Then: '*Jay!*' Even in these circumstances, fury and disillusionment were clear in her voice.

'Go back!' he yelled, recklessly taking one hand off the board to signal shorewards. 'Get off there, go *back*!'

'No!' Her reply came shrilly through the noise of rain and sea, like the call of a gull. '*You* go back! This is nothing to do with you!'

'It is! Robyn, you've got to—'

'*No!*' she shouted again. 'It's Kiran who's got to come for me, don't you understand? It's *got* to be Kiran!'

Jay didn't have the time or the words to tell her that Kiran wouldn't listen and wasn't coming. Waves were rebounding from the Finger to meet and clash with the main tide, and the rescue board lurched and bucked like a wild horse as it was caught between the warring surges. Jay felt sick and dizzy, and his whole body seemed to be on fire with the effort needed to keep some semblance of control.

'Robyn, stop this!' he pleaded. 'We'll talk – we'll all talk! But please, please, don't do this to me!'

The board swung then in a particularly vicious eddy and lurched sideways, almost tipping over. When Jay was able to right it and could look again, Robyn had risen to her feet. She was silhouetted against the sky, a stark, lonely figure on the rock—

And suddenly she wasn't Robyn any more.

Jay nearly fell off the board in shock. *Long hair blowing, long coat flapping, arms outstretched as though to greet the sea* – her head was just a dark shape, her face invisible; rain and spray were blurring his eyes and he knew that what he was seeing wasn't and couldn't be real. *It's an illusion, a waking nightmare, it's got to be, has to be; oh, God, help me . . .*

The flapping coat – *no, it IS an illusion, it IS* – lifted in a gust of wind, flying out to either side of the girl like dark wings. Though he was all but blinded by water and shock and terror, Jay knew that she was staring down at him.

Then her arms arched above her head, her legs bent briefly, and she dived off the end of the rock, into the sea.

Thirteen

I can hear myself screaming, though whether it's aloud or in my head I'll never know. The image of her jumping's burned on my brain as she hits the water, as white spray goes up and she disappears – I've never felt such horror, never felt so helpless and useless and terrified! Another ferocious backwash from the rocks; the board's bucking again, I can't control it, can't see her, can't get to her, and she's going to drown—

'NO!!'

The bellowing voice came from somewhere behind Jay, mingling with the sea's roar. He couldn't turn, dared not do anything that could jeopardize his hold on the rescue board. Then a second long, sleek shape surged into his field of vision, water creaming around it, a figure kneeling, gripping.

'Kiran!' Jay shouted desperately, and let go with one hand for long enough to point. 'Kiran, she's there—'

'I saw!' Kiran's board lurched and almost capsized

as the swell lifted it at a dizzying angle. Kiran clung on; the two boards converged and Jay fought with all his strength to avoid a collision as Kiran made for the spot where Robyn had disappeared.

Something in the water, thrashing – arms flailing, gold hair, *dark hair—*

'There she is!' Jay yelled, then wrenched the rescue board aside as black rock humped above the surface a metre ahead of him. Another wave broke and Kiran caught it; his board swept past Jay, then spun about and raced to the struggling shape. Jay saw Robyn's head come up, glimpsed her face – *but for a split second it's not her face, it's someone else's* – and an arm reaching, desperately clawing. Lightning dazzled his eyes again and he felt its electrical charge shoot through him. Amid the noise of the ensuing thunder he thought he heard someone shriek—

'I've got her, Jay, I've got her!' Kiran was slewed precariously across his board, gripping with toes and one hand, his other hand clamped on Robyn's arm. She turned in the water, kicking, trying to help herself; her other arm came out – *but she's wearing a long-sleeved coat* – flashbacks of a different day, a different rescue, slammed through Jay's head; *but we failed then, we failed – this time we've got to save her, or nothing's worth anything any more!*

'Help me!' Kiran cried. 'She's slipping, I'm losing her!'

His voice broke through the paralysing confusion of the flashbacks. Calling on the last reserves of his energy, Jay forced the rescue board towards him. It shuddered, and a grinding noise came from the underside; in the crazy way that the mind conjures trivia in the middle of an emergency, he thought, *I'm going to owe the surf club a packet after this!* Then another swell did what he couldn't do, flinging the board the last few metres across the gap between them. He and Kiran collided; as the boards rebounded from each other Jay glimpsed a hand, made a blind, desperate grab—

'*Yes!*' Kiran yelled triumphantly. His arm shot out, snatching, heaving. There was a churning and a whirl of bubbles; a dead weight pulled on Jay, nearly tipping him headlong into the sea – *but it's her again, trying to drag us with her like she did before—*

'*Robyn!*' He screamed her name to the sea and the storm as if it were a talisman that could shatter the illusion. Kiran's arm was clamped round her chest, under the armpits; he heaved again, one massive effort, and the rescue board pitched like a roller-coaster as Robyn came up from the water and sprawled across it. Her legs were kicking, hands floundering; her fingers found one of the board's grab-handles and latched on. Then Kiran was there helping her, swinging her unco-ordinated body around and thrusting so that she lay along the board's length with Jay crouched over her. Kiran's eyes were wild, his face white and contorted; gesturing frenetically towards the shore he shouted, '*Go!*'

Jay didn't need to be told twice. He turned his board – how he managed it with the added confusion of Robyn to hamper him he would never know – and steered away from the Finger and the deadly underlying rocks. Waves broke broadside over him and for a moment he thought he would lose his grip; but somehow he hung on, turning again, running with the breakers. Robyn lay beneath him, holding tightly to the grab-handles; he could feel her shuddering and hear her gasping breaths as she cried as though her heart would burst.

Lightning lit up the beach again as he surfed in to shore. Kiran was riding beside him; both boards grounded on sand at the same moment and Jay and Robyn fell off into the shallows. As the undertow pulled back with a hissing, sucking noise, Jay caught Robyn under the arms and dragged her clear of the water.

'I'm all right!' She batted feebly at his hands, sitting up by herself. Tears streamed down her face, but they were indistinguishable from sea- and rainwater. Another figure loomed against the storm-sky and Kiran said in a small, tight voice, 'Is she OK?'

No thanks to you, Jay thought savagely, but kept his feelings from his tone. 'Yeah, I think so. Robyn, if you ever pull a stunt like that again . . .'

The words tailed off as he saw that she was taking no notice of him. She was looking up at Kiran, her expression a mixture of fear, uncertainty and hope. Kiran saw the look and turned away.

'I'll get a thermal blanket from the clubhouse,' he said, distantly.

'I don't need—' Robyn began. But Kiran had already gone.

'Come on,' Jay said gently. 'Can you stand up? Walk a bit?'

She nodded, and let him help her to her feet. Jay had little breath left for saying any more; and besides, what could he say that would serve any purpose at this moment? He wanted to hold Robyn in his arms and comfort her, tell her she was a total idiot but everything would be all right now because he would make it all right. But that wasn't what

Robyn wanted to hear. Or at least, not from him.

Thunder grumbled out over the sea. The rain was still falling like a cataract, but Jay barely noticed it as he helped Robyn towards the clubhouse. It seemed like a long distance; far longer than it should have been. Halfway, they met Kiran returning with a silver package.

'I don't need it,' Robyn said, mulishly. 'I'm fine. Just give me a few minutes.' She looked up. 'You saved me, Kiran. You saved my life.'

Kiran's face closed up. 'It was Jay, not me.'

'It was you,' she insisted. 'It *was*!'

Jay knew what she was trying to do, and pitied her. Over her head, which she had bowed again, he mouthed, 'If she wants to thank you, let her!' But Kiran wouldn't meet his angry gaze. As they walked on towards the clubhouse he kept at a distance. Then suddenly he stopped and looked back. Robyn saw him, and she stopped too, forcing Jay to halt. Kiran was staring towards the Finger. Jay turned his head.

I'll never be sure. What with the near-darkness, and the rain coming down like a curtain, blurring everything . . . but just for one moment I thought there was someone standing on the rock. Someone who held out her arms towards us, like a challenge and a claim . . .

Then a flicker of lightning lit the beach and the empty Finger.

'There's no one there.' Jay heard his own voice as though from a huge distance. 'Hear what I'm saying, Kiran? No one. There never was.'

The scene lit up again briefly. Kiran blinked and pinched the bridge of his nose between finger and thumb. He looked as if he might say something, but changed his mind and kept it to himself.

In the clubhouse, Jay tried to make Robyn sit down and be looked after. But Robyn was having none of it.

'I keep telling you, I'm fine,' she said, flatly. 'I'm going to have a shower.' Her eyes roamed the room then dwelled on Kiran. 'Wait for me, yes?'

Jay said, 'Of course,' but Kiran said nothing. Robyn disappeared into the cubicle and, as the sound of the shower began, Kiran walked outside. Jay followed, and found him standing on the sand and staring seawards again. There was a question in Jay's mind, and however much Kiran might dislike it, he wasn't going to be satisfied until he had an answer.

He said: 'Just now, out there ... Who did you think we were rescuing?'

Kiran turned and looked at him. 'What kind of a stupid . . .' But he didn't finish.

'Yeah.' Jay understood. 'It wasn't Robyn, was it? Not in your mind.' *And what was in your mind was so strong that it infected me, too.* 'She's dead, Kiran. She's been dead since the day we failed to save her. She didn't come back. It wasn't real.'

Kiran said bitterly, 'You don't know anything!'

Oh, but I do. 'If there's a ghost,' Jay went on, 'then you created it. Isn't it time to stop? For Robyn's sake, as well as yours?'

But as lightning illuminated Kiran's face, Jay realized that Robyn's sake had no part to play. Maybe what had happened would 'cure' Kiran of his belief that he had been haunted. Jay didn't know. But as to what the ghost represented . . . that was something else entirely. It was the focus for a feeling within Kiran that Jay could not penetrate or share or truly understand. An unsolvable mystery, an unknown and unattainable ideal. The elusive fantasy of what might have been.

Something had ended tonight. Kiran's obsession? Yes, possibly. But something else, too. Jay looked at Kiran again and saw a stranger. The old, familiar Kiran had moved aside and made way for – well, perhaps not a different person. But changed. And the old Kiran would not be coming back.

Kiran scuffed with one foot at the sand beneath his feet. 'I'm going to get dressed,' he said.

'Yeah.' Practical things, down to earth. It was the only option, really. Jay stayed where he was as Kiran disappeared into the clubhouse. Robyn would be out of the shower soon; he'd leave them alone for a few minutes, in case they wanted to talk. Though he didn't think they would.

I feel so sad. Never felt anything quite like it before, and I don't know what it's all about. It's as if I've lost something, and it was very important to me, but I can't even remember what it is.

He looked, one last time, towards the Finger, remembering those few horrifying minutes when the sea was churning around him and the rocks were lethally close and he thought that Robyn was going to die. *What did I really see? The hair, the coat . . . was it Robyn? Did she play the part and play it so well that I was taken in by it, too? She did it for Kiran. But maybe she did it for herself, too. Maybe there was a ghost of her own, and it had to be exorcised.*

He stood in the rain, thinking. The lightning and thunder were less frequent now; the worst of the storm had stayed out to sea and was moving slowly up coast. Tiredness was like a fog in his mind and he knew he desperately needed sleep. But right now, he felt as if he would never sleep again.

A soft sound behind him, and Kiran emerged from the clubhouse. He had changed into jeans and hooded top, and had his dripping wetsuit flung over one shoulder.

'I'm going home,' he said.

Jay nodded.

'Robyn's in there. She's dressed. See her back to her place, OK?'

'Aren't you . . .' But Jay left the question unfinished. *Something's ended tonight* . . . 'Sure,' he said quietly, 'I'll look after her.'

'Yeah. You always would have done, wouldn't you?' Kiran pushed a hand through his wet hair. 'Right. I'll call you sometime. Or see you around.'

Another nod. Jay couldn't think of anything to say. He watched Kiran walk to the beach steps, up them, and his figure diminish along the road. No one else in sight; no one venturing out in weather like this. *Except us. Idiots that we are.*

Robyn was sitting on the clubhouse bench. Her hands were loose in her lap and she was staring at the floor as though it mattered.

'Hi.' Jay moved to stand beside her.

'Hi.' No expression whatever in her voice.

'You OK?'

'Yup.' Then, Robynish: 'Fighting fit, that's me.'

'I'm going to walk you home.'

'There's no need.'

'There is. Anyway, I promised Kiran.'

'Ah. Can't let Kiran down, can we?' Her lower lip trembled. 'Oh, Jay . . .'

He sat down and for only the second time in her life she let him hold her, pressing her face against his chest. She didn't cry; that time had passed and she had moved on to something beyond it, something harder and tougher and more controlled. After perhaps a minute she drew away from him, stood up and took a deep breath, straightening her shoulders.

Jay gazed at her. In a way, the gesture she had just made was a greater rejection than if she had pushed him away. She needed comfort, that was all, and because he was here and was offering, she had accepted it from him. But it didn't mean anything to her. It never had, and never would.

You wanted to be Kiran's merrow, Robyn. I don't think you were. I think she was – is – someone else, and Kiran hasn't found her yet. But I've got a merrow of my own, and it's you. I wish I could tell you that. I won't though, because I haven't got the courage. And that's another thing that has 'never' attached to it.

He felt the sadness come welling up again. 'Why did you do it, Robyn? Did you truly think—'

'I don't know.' She cut across him, not wanting to hear the rest. 'But . . . I'm glad I did, in a way. I suppose it's achieved something.' She smiled crookedly, jerkily. 'Story to tell my grandkids, fifty years from now.'

He laughed despite himself; or maybe it was the only way he had of relieving a little of the tension. 'You won't change,' he said.

'You think so? I don't. I *have* changed, Jay. Everything has, whether we like it or not. Ohhh . . .' She waved a hand irritably and grimaced. 'This isn't exactly the best time to start spouting philosophy, is it? My hair's wet, and I didn't dry off after the shower so my clothes are wet too, and I'm starting to feel bloody cold.' She moved to the door. 'I'm going now. Walk with me, if you want to.'

Yeah. For all the good it'll do, I want to . . . Robyn was right when she said everything had changed. Yet in a way she was wrong, too. Some things never would be any different, however much he might want them to be.

He looked at her, and for a moment all the

emotion in him, his feelings towards her, showed in his face. Her head was turned away and she didn't see the look. *That's all right. She wasn't meant to; it wouldn't be fair.*

'Come on, if you're coming,' Robyn said.

He switched off the clubhouse lights and closed the door behind them. The rain had slackened off to a drizzle now and the street lamps had come on. The falling water sparkled in the lamplight like wavering haloes. Jay took Robyn's hand; she held it for a moment, squeezing his fingers, then gently pulled away.

She went ahead of him up the steps, and at the top she paused, looking along the road. Jay knew whom she was hoping to see. But no one else was waiting for her.

They walked together in the direction of the harbour, and neither had anything to say.

A note from the author

The Cornish sea has many moods
and is never entirely predictable.
One stormy day in St. Ives, I watched its
colour change in minutes, from gentle turquoise
through intense sapphire to dangerous grey.
Just the way people can suddenly change.
And that's how this story began.

Louise Cooper is the author of countless
fantasy novels, for both adults and
children, but MERROW is her first
fabulous book for Bite.